Jessie Sale (Hopkins) Lloyd

**We Costelions.**

A Novel: Vol. I.

Jessie Sale (Hopkins) Lloyd

**We Costelions.**
*A Novel: Vol. I.*

ISBN/EAN: 9783337051457

Printed in Europe, USA, Canada, Australia, Japan

Cover: Foto ©Andreas Hilbeck / pixelio.de

More available books at **www.hansebooks.com**

# WE COSTELIONS.

## A Novel.

BY

## J. SALE LLOYD,

AUTHOR OF

"THE SILENT SHADOW," "RUTH EVERINGHAM," "THE HAZELHURST
MYSTERY," "RAGAMUFFINS," ETC., ETC.,
AND EDITOR OF "SHADOWS OF THE PAST."

IN THREE VOLUMES.

## VOL. I.

LONDON:
TINSLEY BROTHERS, 8, CATHERINE ST., STRAND.
1882.

LONDON:
STEVENS & RICHARDSON, PRINTERS, 5, GREAT QUEEN STREET,
LINCOLN'S INN FIELDS, W.C.

TO

## HER DEAR MOTHER

(HER FIRST CRITIC, AND EVER KIND HELPER)

# These Pages

ARE LOVINGLY DEDICATED

BY

## THE AUTHOR.

# CONTENTS.

---

## VOL. I.

# WE COSTELIONS.

## CHAPTER I.

WE Costelions are rather an intricate
family to write about, nevertheless I will
endeavour to tell the story of our lives,
as far as it is known to me, and dear Aunt
Phillis's work among us.

We pride ourselves greatly upon our
blue blood, and hold up our heads because
our family tree carries our name from the
present time back to that of the Conqueror.
I doubt if we are great favourites; it seems
to run in our natures to be overbearing

and intolerant. We are born proud, I
verily believe, and I, being the eldest, have
had some opportunities of judging.

The Costelion babies have always kicked
and screamed as no other babies I have
ever seen, and the small children would go
their own way as soon as their tiny feet
could toddle.

At the time of which I write, we were
still living in our dear old Devonshire
home, some twelve miles from the picturesque town of Kingsbridge.

No trains came into our lovely country
to disturb us with their noise and smoke;
the turmoil of railway speed kept far away
from our dear Kingsholme.

No telegrams came near us; even in
these days of electricity, our tiny world
was calm and peaceful, when we kept our
Costelion tempers governed.

Kingsholme Abbey was the name of the

beloved old place, which had been in our family for many generations.

It stood out upon the high rocks, a landmark to those at sea, yet we were sheltered from the blasts of the wind by ground far higher, which rose above us covered with verdant brushwood, ferns, and wildflowers, where the white-tailed rabbits ran by thousands, or sunned themselves on the soft grass.

My father's preserves these were, in which I have spent many an hour, well nigh lost among the tangled ivy with my book, or looking out upon the varied hues of the sea, while the beautiful golden-brown pheasants rose at sight of me with their strange, startling cry.

The soft breezes came to us briny and refreshing, straight from the open sea, and from the Abbey windows we witnessed many a fearful storm, ourselves sheltered and snug.

Before our home lay smooth, mossy, green lawns and beds of brilliant flowers, while the arbutus bore its wax-like blossom and its bright red fruit, and the myrtles bloomed freely in the open air, and the oranges and citrons hung their golden fruits upon our walls, ripened by the summer sun, and the grass went sloping down to the rugged rocks, among which were some winding steps to the water's edge.

We had no sands at Kingsholme, but the sea-washed pebbles and shells were treasures to us in our childhood, and the seaweeds, too, we collected and spread out on the pages of books which we had for the purpose; but what we delighted most in was our boat, which was moored in a little bay, where the bright shingle lay fine and many-coloured.

We used no machine when we bathed at Kingsholme; we all had our bathing-dresses, the same as are used at French watering-places, and we girls went out daily swimming with our brothers in summer time, and fishing with them, too, for the matter of that, and paddling with our pink feet among the white crests of the waves, or upon the slippery, weed-covered rocks.

Now that these things are past, I like to look back on those days in the dear old home.

How picturesque it was, with its time-tinted grey walls, patches of golden lichens, and tiny green ferns! The ceterach and asplenium ruta muraria nestled between the rough old stones; the polypodium vulgare and asplenium trichomanes, or common maidenhair spleenwort, also took root among its ancient masonry, while the time-honoured ivy half covered its walls, and peeped in at the windows; and the

birds built their nests among the thick-
sheltering leaves, and sang to us all the
summer through, claiming payment in the
cold days of winter, when they found food
scarce, in the shape of crumbs. To the
left of our home lay a large bay, at the
further extent of which was Kingsbridge,
with its many spires, heaven-pointed—
the white houses showing in bright relief
against the dark trees which formed its
background, while on either side of the
broad bay were the dwellings and estates
of our friends and neighbours.

This was our world.

Our own household consisted of my
father, Sir Charteris Costelion ; his mother,
old Lady Costelion ; my brother Charteris
(known among us only as Bob, except
when our father spoke of him) ; Trevelyan,
our second boy, and Florence, our father's
darling, and, indeed, the pet of the whole

family, who came between my two brothers; and, lastly, myself, my father's first-born and least-loved child.

Grandmamma Costelion was a stately old dame, a Devereux by birth, whose French mother had been immured in the Bastile for writing some book, innocent in itself, but held to be dangerous in those days, when freedom of thought was not admissible, and our grandmamma, like her mother, was a highly educated woman, who had been known in the literary world in her day, but that day had long gone by, and we found her learning somewhat troublesome to us in her old age.

Our father had been born in our dear home, Kingsholme Abbey, and had inherited it from his father, as well as the baronetcy. He had, however, by no means always lived there, for he had in his youth preferred lamp-posts to trees, town to

country. Everyone said Sir Charteris
Costelion was a man made for society, and
in society he lived. Before the death of
his father he had fallen in love with and
had wished to marry a young girl, the
daughter of a Devonshire neighbour, who
was a man of good birth and small means,
but neither family would hear of the
match, although his love was recipro-
cated.

My grandfather had been a man of
fashion, and had lived far beyond his in-
come ; he could leave his son his name
and entailed estate, but simply nothing
to keep it up on.

He told my father that a rich wife only
could save his name from ruin, and a rich
wife was therefore found for him.

That was my mother and Bob's. She
was, I believe, the daughter of some
wealthy London merchant, and greatly

the Costelions looked down upon her; but her money was good, although it had been earned by trade, and they spent it.

My father is a handsome man now, but I am told that he was eminently handsome in his youth, and people say that my mother loved him with a rare affection; but love does not come at will, and Sir Charteris never cared for his wife. Three years after her marriage she died, here, at Kingsholme Abbey.

I can scarcely remember her. I was only two years old when I lost her, and yet it seems to me I have a faint memory of a beautiful, anxious face, framed in dark, luxuriant hair, with loving brown eyes, leaning over me—a pale, sad face, if I remember it rightly. I think, too, I recollect that she kissed me, and that my young cheeks were wet with her tears; yet I was only two years old. Perhaps, after all, these things are merely fancy.

My father says that I am like my mother, though I am plainer. They all call me plain, and I suppose I am so.

When I look into my glass I see a dark-skinned, dark-eyed, dark-haired, dark-browed girl, with a wistful look gazing back at me. The face I see *is* like my mother's (if I really remember her, and have not drawn a mental picture of her), and like her's it is a sad face, wanting something, surely—what is that something? Is it love?

Well, perhaps.

No one cares much for Miriam Costelion, that I know. Sometimes I am called "You brown little girl," or referred to as "a brown patch," and to add to my sin of ugliness, I am small, while all the Costelions are tall and well made.

When I was *very* young these remarks made me suffer; after that they hardened me.

They all used to say I was not a Costelion; they would not own me. I took after my mother, and, like her, was only an Armatage.

I think in those days my mother's memory was about the only thing really dear to me, and that I reverenced greatly from childhood. I have often sat looking out to sea, and fancying her doing so before me. The room in which she died I had taken for my own; it was only used for lumber, no one cared to sleep there, and so I begged for it. I was wondered at and laughed at; but as no one else wanted it my request was granted, and my mother's room became mine.

My father was fond of Bob because he resembled himself. He was a thorough Costelion, although he had the misfortune

of having Armatage blood in his veins too :
but he bore his name and was his heir; no
wonder my father thought a great deal of
Bob. I was fond of him also, but I think
it was because he was my mother's son.

In those days I fear I had not very right
feelings in my heart towards my father,
and indeed towards all of my family. I
was somewhat antagonistic. I resented
their want of love for me; it made me hard
and unnatural.

As I have said, my mother died—Bob's
mother and mine.

She left my father all her fortune. She
loved him, and withheld nothing from him,
not even to secure on her own children.

My father has spent it like a Costelion;
but he had only made a small hole in it
during my mother's lifetime, there was
therefore no need of another rich wife to
prop up the tottering honour of his family.

My mother had been sacrificed—that was enough. So my father offered again to his old love, and this time her family did not say him nay, as Kingsholme Abbey had become his, and his first wife's money was sufficient to keep it up. And not more than a year after my mother had been carried out of the dear old home, another mistress was brought to reign there.

There is even now a full-length portrait of my father's second wife at Kingsholme Abbey. Young as I was, I can well re-member her coming among us. She might have been born a Costelion herself, with her curling, scornful lip, and disdainful blue eyes; yet she was marvellously handsome. Her hair was like sun-rays, with a warm red tinge in it; her complexion purest white, with the most delicate bloom.

My father loved his second wife; he was strangely tender with her—for him. I have

watched them often strolling arm in arm
down those paths among the flowers where
my mother's coffin had passed, only a year
before, and, child though I was, my heart
was bitter against them, for her sake.   He
had never wandered thus with *her* among
the roses and the myrtle blossoms.

I did not love my stepmother, I know,
nor did my stepmother love me.   The first
time she saw me she despised me.

"Surely, Charteris, this ugly, dark little
wretch is not your child?" she had said, in
her scornful voice; and I had seen my
father's brow flush with shame of me.

I have never forgotten that, and at the
time I thought I should never forgive it.

But my father's joy did not last very
long: he and his beautiful wife got tired
of the dear old home, and went away to
travel.

It was about two years after their marriage that the news came to us that she was dead. She had fallen a victim to Roman fever at Tivoli. Neither Bob nor I pretended to be very sorry; we had never loved our stepmother, and I know, wicked as it was, I felt really glad I should not see her again. We two children had run very wild in those days when we had been left alone, and we heard with awe that our father was coming back to the Abbey, for we were somewhat afraid of him.

When he arrived he brought an Italian nurse with him, and a lovely, fair child. It was my sister Florence; she was a year old, but my father had not thought it necessary to let us know of her birth.

What an exquisite babe she was, like a tender blush rosebud; and little as I had loved her mother, I took the child at once into my heart, and from our earliest acquaintance my sister Florence has made me her slave. It was strange I should care for her when she so strongly resembled my step-mother, and that when I heard my father call us "beauty and the beast," I still loved my little sister.

As for my father, he worshipped her as he had worshipped her mother before her. And as she grew she was allowed her own way in everything; even her father, who we all feared, gave way to her.

Yes! Florence was a thorough Costelion!

As I look back upon her childhood, how many of her proud little ways come to me; how well I remember her being presented with her first prayer-book, and what she said upon the occasion.

It was no easy matter to get to church from Kingsholme Abbey. It meant a twenty-four mile drive; for my father always went to Kingsbridge when he was at home (which was not very often after my stepmother died), driving there in a " break " with four fine stepping horses.

When he was away no one went from our house ; he would have thought it a most unnecessary proceeding to have out a carriage to send *us*. It was quite the right thing for the *head of the family* to show himself every Sunday, but for us it mattered little whether we went to church or no.

My father used to take me with him sometimes, ugly as I was, and Bob too ; but Florence had never been, she was so young. She did not at all like being left behind, and often I stayed too to comfort her. Father had promised that as soon as she was four years old she should go to her first service ; in the interim my little sister was always asking me to tell her what it would be like, and I did my best to enlighten her from my own limited store of knowledge. I told her that there was an organ, and that a man played upon it, at which Florence nodded her bright head approvingly. But, alas! I never reflected that the only organ my sister had ever seen was a hand organ in the streets of Kingsbridge! I spoke to her of the choir, and described how little boys, dressed in white, came out of a room, and walked along, two and two, and sang. At this Florence looked thoughtful. She had seen nothing of that sort; it was at present a mystery which was to be revealed the first Sunday after her fourth birthday, when she was to be the proud possessor of a prayer-book all to herself. Many and many a talk we had about that book, picturing its anticipated beauties; and when at length my sister's birthday came, the book which my father gave her was far more beautiful than any *I* had ever seen, but it did not please Florence.

It was ivory bound, and on its side there was a cross of brass, under which was printed "Common Prayer."

Now Grandmamma Costelion was a martinet upon the subject of education, and even at four years old Florence could read, and read well, and when she saw these words upon her prayer-book she burst into passionate tears.

"Oh!" she cried, "I won't have a *common* prayer-book; I want a *best* one! Oh! it is unkind of you, papa, to buy me a *common* one!"

Ah! my sister Florence, you wanted even the name of the prayer-book to be changed for you.

The long talked of Sunday came; the day was fine, and we drove to Kingsbridge.

Florence looked very lovely with the flush of excitement upon her fair young face.

My father placed her next him, and I sat on the other side of her.

What a contrast they looked ; this small creature of four beside that majestic form ; for my father was some six feet one or two inches high, broad and well made, with a proud stern face and a haughty manner. He was very fond of his little daughter, but it would have been beneath his dignity to speak to her, or, indeed, to any one in church, so the tug at his sleeve was disregarded.

The prayer in the vestry was ended, and the choristers sang their response, "*Amen.*" In a moment Florence was standing upon the seat, peering over the church with an eager face. "Did you hear, papa? they said 'coming!'"

She was very quiet and interested as they filed in two and two, but when this ceremony was over, she exclaimed, "Why !

they've got their night dresses on, I declare!"

I knew she ought not to be standing up there on the seat, but I was afraid to tell her not to do it, for Florence always had her own way.

I could see by my father's face that he was annoyed, but he would not own a Costelion to be in the wrong, even though that Costelion was but a little child.

So he paid no heed to the small rebel, whose outspoken words made me crimson, and set Bob off laughing, and caused those near us to smile. I knelt down and tried not to look at her; the organ was playing. The service began, and for a while she was still; then, in a pause, her shrill voice rang out—

"Miriam, what a big organ! where's the man who plays it?"

"Oh! hush, Florrie," then, in a hurried

whisper, I add, "he's behind that red curtain."

"And where's the *monkey?* Is he there, too?" Bob laughs out; I stuff my hand-kerchief into my mouth, and grow scarlet. My father turns an angry glance on us, and with one strong hand I am whisked to the other side of him into the corner of the pew. It is me with whom he is vexed— not Florence. I sit there not daring to ask for my book; I am afraid to look up. I know my father is annoyed with me, yet why? What have I done? I resent his anger, and do not listen to a word of the service—instead I think hard thoughts of my father, and his want of love for me; I shall never forget that scene in church!

After that I preferred staying at home and wandering in the garden or climbing the rocks. I loved all nature even in those days, but I then thought nothing of nature's God when looking upon the beauties around me.

The soft down on the butterfly's wing was to me very beautiful and marvellous, but it did not suggest to me the gentleness of the Great Maker.

I used to watch the storms at sea, and the lightning gliding serpent-like along the water, and I thought them grand and glorious, but failed to see in them the power of God.

Now, each tree and flower, each bird and gauzy-winged summer fly, each wondrous snowflake and crystal dewdrop, speaks to me of its maker. And for all that is better in me since those days, I have to thank Aunt Phillis.

But I am anticipating.

I was piecing together the memories of my childhood, in those days when Aunt Phillis's sweet face had not entered into my life. I must take up the thread where I dropped it, and tell of the change which came to us in our old home.

My father married a third wife. Why, I doubt if he could have told you himself.

My second stepmother was a lady in her own right, so perhaps that was the reason he married her. She was a silly " feckless " creature, with no thoughts beyond her dress and what was the latest fashion.

She had no authority over us children, and old Lady Costelion kept her under her thumb. A woman of iron will was our grandmamma, as we sometimes found out to our cost.

Well! Trevelyan was the only child of the third Lady Costelion, and was named after her family.

We were not improved in any way by the arrival of our new stepmother. She soon wearied of the dear old home, and longed to be among her fashionable friends again; to drive in the "Row," and listen to the unmeaning flatteries of her London acquaintances. Dear old Kingsholme was not in her line at all.

Poor Lady Lavinia! I fear we Costelions led her a miserable life between us all; she could not stand up against our wild spirits.

We never thought of obeying her in any one way.

We of course saw our neighbours, and called them friends; we led the society for a long radius round Kingsbridge. We were looked up to, no doubt, but most people were afraid of us and our proud ways and cutting speeches.

Yes! looking back, I firmly believe we Costelions were hated, and I am not sure we did not deserve it, for we never thought of any one's pleasure but our

own. We were Costelions, and that was
enough.

I do not care to recall our neighbours of
those days (save one family), they were
nothing to us, nor we to them. But that
one I must speak of.

Some half mile down the bay lived
Colonel Armstrong ; he and my father did
not get on very well together, so that we
were never on intimate terms with the
family, who were not Devonshire people,
and only came to live there when I was
about fifteen years of age. I was accustomed to the management of a boat, but I
did not often go out alone. Bob was generally ready to accompany me, but to my
great sorrow he had at this period been
sent off to Eton.

So one day I got into the little craft,
and started for a sail by myself.

We Costelions have no fear, and no

nervous systems—we were born without, I think.

I enjoyed the sail out greatly, but the wind became so strong that I found it hard work to manage the boat; I did my best to get home, but could not fetch the point required; the wind drove me with fury past the old Abbey house down the bay.

I turned about, jibing the sail; the wind caught it, and in another moment I was in the water, for the boat had capsized. I felt the immersion, but after that things were very vague to me. I suppose I must have been struck in the overturning of my little boat.

The first fact that I became aware of was that a kind face was leaning over me, and the intense gaze of a pair of honest blue eyes was fixed upon me, and somehow I felt secure.

I know I did not speak, and I do not

think I had fairly recovered my senses, for I closed my eyes again without a question as to why those strong arms were around me, and I must have relapsed into insensibility, for when I again opened them I found myself lying on a sofa wrapped in fur rugs, while my hands and feet were being rubbed diligently.

"Thank God!" murmured the owner of the blue eyes, as I looked about me.

"Come, that's better," said a hearty voice, while a fine soldierly looking man came to my side and smiled upon me.

"Where am I?" I asked dreamily.

"You are all safe, my dear, and among friends," answered a gentle-faced woman, who held my hands between her own, and chafed them with her soft palm. "You have had a little accident, but it is all right now."

I looked at the young man with the

honest eyes, and saw that he was wet through, and remembered how he had borne me in his arms.

"Yes, I recollect, I upset the boat;" and then I turned to him. "Did you save me?" I asked.

"I was permitted that privilege," he replied, with a kindly smile.

"You risked your life for mine," I answered; "it was very good of you, and yet I am not grateful. I think I am tired of living" (then with energy)— "Oh! where is the boat, what became of it?"

"I do not know; I was thinking only of you."

"Oh! how angry papa will be; why, why did you not save it instead of me?" I asked passionately.

He leant over me and answered in a low voice, but the words went straight to my

heart, and many an after-day I heard their
echo.

" Because, Miss Costelion, it had no life,
and *no immortal soul.*"

No one had spoken to me before of my
soul; his words came to me with a shock,
and for a moment I was silenced; but then
my Costelion blood arose, and I replied,
" Nevertheless, I wish you had left me and
towed the boat on shore."

" And you think that would have pleased
your father?" (in a sad tone).

" Why not? I am ugly; what does he
care for me?"

" A great deal, I should say : however, if
it will make you happier, I will try and
rescue your boat;" and before I could
answer him he was gone, and somehow I
felt as if the sun had ceased to shine; but
I had not much time for thinking, as the
doctor had been sent for and had arrived.

He ordered me to bed at once, and undertook to go to my father himself and explain the accident which had occurred, and also to promise him that Colonel and Mrs. Armstrong would take every care of me.

I grew hot and cold as I listened, for well I knew that the fact of my being under their roof would incense him greatly; but what could I do? The doctor threatened me with rheumatic fever if I did not obey his orders implicitly; then there was that sweet motherly face smiling on me, and I remembered the kind look in those honest blue eyes, and I determined to stay.

Mrs. Armstrong put me to bed herself, and waited on me—no one else entered my room. I became feverishly anxious about my preserver—he had saved me, and I had been ungrateful. I had, even by my words, driven him forth to risk his life a second time for me, just on the chance of finding an old boat, at most worth only a few pounds. And why? simply to save me from the scolding which I well deserved.

The gentle mother's face wore an anxious look as evening drew on. I longed to ask if her son had returned; yet somehow I dared not, for I felt that my conduct had been wrong and selfish. At length, when she bade me good night, I could refrain no longer, and I whispered my question.

"No, my dear, Herbert has not come back. Yes; we feel anxious, but he is as dear to our Heavenly Father as he is to us, and He will watch over him."

I was silenced and awed; I could not answer her; I had never heard anyone speak thus before. She kissed me upon the forehead and went out quietly, and I was left alone.

Sleep would not come to me.

In every shriek of the wind I heard my preserver crying for help.

Many times I sprang out of bed at the risk of making myself ill, and stood at the window looking out into the blackness of the night.

"Oh! if he would only come back!" I repeated monotonously. "If he would only come back!" But he came not.

The wind howled on, the sea roared, and I strained my ears to listen to every sound. At length the morning dawned, and I crept back to my bed with an aching heart, and, utterly weary, I fell asleep. When I awoke the sun was streaming into my chamber window, and in its glory stood— yes! it was a woman—it was my kind hostess; but for the first moment of my awaking, her sweet gentle face seemed to me that of an angel.

"Our son has returned, Miss Costelion. He sends you a message to say that your boat is safe. It had drifted up the bay, as he had expected, so he was fortunate enough to find it, and has towed it to shore."

What could I answer?

My mind was wearied with much watching; my body weakened by the fright and the chill; my nerves had been strung at full tension, and the relief from anxiety, mingled with the unlooked for kindness, was too much for me. I burst into tears— I, Miriam Costelion!

"My dear," said Mrs. Armstrong, gently, "what is the matter?"

"Oh! Mrs. Armstrong, I have been so wrong, so ungrateful, so wicked, and I am miserable," I sobbed.

"Dear child, if you feel this to be the case, you need not be unhappy. You know where to seek and find forgiveness."

Well, yes! I suppose I knew as much as that. I had been told so before in church; but the words found no response in my heart.

It did not come easy to me to ask for forgiveness. I was a Costelion.

"Your son has been very good to me," I said, in a subdued voice.

A bright look came over the mother's face.

"Only we who know him well, and his God, know *how* good," she answered.

Then, after a pause, she handed me a letter, and went away to get me my breakfast. I broke the envelope open and read :

"DEAR MIRIAM,

"I am greatly annoyed that your imprudence should have got you into such a disagreeable scrape. It is most vexing to me to have you under the roof of a man whom I do not like, and do not intend to visit.

I desire that you should return home as soon as possible.

"Affectionately yours,

" CHARTERIS COSTELION."

Angry tears sprung to my eyes. This, then, was all that he had to say when his child had been rescued from a watery grave! No, not a word of thanks to my preserver even! I would *not* obey him; I would *not* go home; I would remain with my new found friends as long as I liked. And I tore my father's letter into a thousand fragments.

I did remain on with Colonel and Mrs. Armstrong. Had I stayed long enough, and had they known me better, my visit to them could not have failed to do me good. As it was, I saw that they thought me ill-used, unkindly treated, and to be pitied, and I accepted their sympathy. I had not then learned that to gain love a child must be gentle and humble. That lesson I was taught by Aunt Phillis. I saw a great deal of my preserver, Herbert Armstrong. He was very good to me, kind and thoughtful; but I fear I shocked him sometimes when I spoke of my father; yet his evident sorrow seemed to make him more tender over me.

One day when I had been talking as I know now I ought not to have done, on looking up I saw Herbert Armstrong's blue eyes fixed upon me.

"Miriam," he said (they had all learnt to call me by my Christian name), "Miriam, are you right to judge your father?"

I raised my head, meaning to justify myself, but when I looked into his earnest face, I could not; and instead of answering, my eyes fell before his, while deep down in my heart I knew he was right ; but I was too proud to acknowledge it, so I turned the subject.

Ah! that was a good time I spent with the Armstrongs, but it could not last for ever : my father ascertained from the medical man that I was perfectly well again, and the same day he wrote his thanks to my host and hostess, a handsome present of game accompanying his letter, and within a few hours the " Abbey carriage " was standing at the door awaiting me.

My father was very angry with me for having disobeyed his orders ; then, I considered, most unjustly so, and I kept up war with him.

He forbade my going to the Armstrongs' house, thinking they had retained me, knowing his wishes ; but they did not know them, and very sure I am that they would not have asked me to remain had they been aware of them.

I used to steal away sometimes and go and sit on a low stool at Mrs. Armstrong's feet; but I had seldom much to say when there, for I knew I was doing wrong.

And often Herbert and I met on the rocks by the shore, or among the pine trees and the tangled undergrowth, and walked together side by side.

I was generally silent then : my heart seemed very full, yet the truth was veiled from me.

Herbert Armstrong was no great talker either, and sometimes I noticed a far-off saddened look in his face, and wondered at it, but that was all.

Old Lady Costelion's mantle had descended upon me. I was very fond of scribbling. One day Herbert found me sitting in a cave writing a poem to the ocean. I tried to hide it at first, but when I found he really wished to read it I handed it to him without another word.   He went through it attentively, and then looked up at me with his rare smile.

"Miriam, if you will to become an authoress, the power of writing is in you."

I flushed with pleasure at his praise, and never complained that he forgot to return the verses I had composed.   But my happiness quickly faded when he told me that he was going out to India at once to join the regiment to which he had been appointed, for he had made up his mind to follow his father's profession.

That was our good bye.   I did not know why I was so sorry at his going, or why our hands lingered in that last clasp, or wherefore, as I watched his retreating form, my vision became dim with tears.

·I turned slowly, going homewards as a wounded bird seeks its nest, not realising where my hurt was, but feeling its sharp pain.

I did not see Herbert Armstrong again. I could not even comfort myself with his parents—they had gone to see their son off, after which they were to travel.

Just at this time our life was not greatly improved by the death of our step-mother's father, Lord Trevelyan. The estates went, of course, to the eldest son, and the Dowager Lady Trevelyan had to turn out for the new marchioness.

The Trevelyans were very poor, and the dower settled upon the old lady was not large. My step-mother wished to have her to live at Kingsholme Abbey, and my father consented. He was a generous man, and thought nothing of the expense, and not being much at home himself he hoped his wife would be less lonely if her mother were with her.

So she came; and a strange hypochondriacal woman was Lady Trevelyan. She seemed to be really in perfect health, but complained of every disease under the sun.

She had been a beauty in her time; but her day had long gone by, and she was brown and thin.

We made a great trouble of having the old lady among us; but then we hardly knew what trouble was: we still had the lesson to learn, and this is how it came to us.

One morning the post-bag was brought in as usual and laid on the breakfast table beside my father's plate. He opened it and distributed the letters.

There was one for Lady Costelion—I mean our grandmamma—and one for Lady Trevelyan, and several for himself.

It was easy to see that some great blow had fallen upon them all three, and it was

strange to note how differently each bore
it. Grandmamma Costelion sat erect as
though turned to stone; not a word
escaped her lips, and her eyes had a fixed
hard look in them. My father sprung to
his feet, and gazed wildly about him, but
asked sympathy of none.

Lady Trevelyan's thin brown hands
trembled as she held the fatal missive, and
she made her moan in a wailing, pitiful
voice, " Lavinia, the bank has failed! We
have lost everything; and oh! my dear, I
shall be a burthen upon you in my old age.
Oh! I am so sorry, Lavinia, my dear—a
marchioness and a beggar! Well, well, I
have not long to live; in my state of
health I shall not trouble you long, and
beggar though I am, dear Sir Charteris is
rich, and he will not turn me out."

" No, I will not turn you out "—from
my father—" but I too have lost all ! "

" You.   How ? "

" The bank failure which has ruined you has done the same to me," answered my father, with dignity.

" Oh ! what will you do, Charteris ? " asked my stepmother, anxiously.

" I shall work, I suppose, if any one will employ me," said my father, bitterly.  " The Costelions' day is past."

I had not loved my father, but my heart went out to him in his sorrow.  I placed my small sunburnt hand upon his well-formed aristocratic white one, and said, " The darkest cloud has sometimes a silver lining, papa ! "  I was afraid when I had spoken, but he did not answer me.  I looked into his face, it was grave and thoughtful.  I felt for the first time in my life proud of my father ; he was bearing his trouble like a man.

Grandmamma Costelion now spoke.

" I do not wish to be a nuisance to anyone ; I shall go to the Union."

" You will go there when I do, mother,
but not before," said my father, firmly.

" Well, at any rate we can never be
beggars," said Florence, proudly. " We
shall always be the Costelions of Kingsholme Abbey, whether you have lost your
money or no papa ; our position is un-
deniable."

" We must leave Kingsholme Abbey,"
said my father, quietly.

" Leave Kingsholme Abbey ? leave our
home ? " cried my sister, aghast.

And my heart sank as I listened.

" Yes ! Florence ; how do you suppose
I could keep it up ? It is all I have
left. I must take some small house and
let this."

I shuddered.

" Let this ! oh ! papa, when the Costelions have lived here from generation to generation."

"Well, my dear, I don't suppose they will ever live here again."

"No! some snobs will take the place who have made their money by candles or blacking," exclaimed Florence, bitterly.

"Whoever will give the highest price must rent it; that is all we shall have to live on. The boys must come back from Eton; it is a pity, but it can't be helped," said my father.

And so the curtain fell upon our old life.

# CHAPTER II.

I DO not think there was ever a lovelier home in all England than Kingsholme Abbey. It was hard to realize leaving it when that calamity was but a name to us.

There were many houses doubtless better and more richly furnished belonging to the merchant and city princes of the day, but none could have been more picturesque than our own, either inside or out. Even the well-worn carpets had only become softened and subdued in colour by time. The old Chippendale furniture in our breakfast-room would not easily be procured now, nor the rich dark carved oak of our dining-room, nor the suite of veritable " Queen Ann's " which our drawing-room contained.

The lights and shadows everywhere to be found at the Abbey, coming to us mellow through the diamond window panes, would never be ours to enjoy again in one of the lath and plaister villas which must be our place of habitation in future.

I never dreamed how weak I was with regard to our old home until I knew that I must leave it. I thought that being a Costelion I could not fail to be strong, but I suppose my plebeian Armatage blood demoralized me. Florence complained bitterly, and was very angry with every one for the misfortune which had befallen us, but she did not seem to feel as I did the breaking up of all the dear old associations of our " dulce domum."

No more should I be able to sit and gaze

out upon the troubled sea, no more picture my mother seated in the chair which somehow I had learned had been her favourite ; no more in fancy see her dear face bending over the very books in the library which bore her name, or writing at the little table which had been hers. All these thoughts of her must be snapped. I did not feel that I could think them away from her presence-haunted rooms. My own bedchamber, which had been hers, was perhaps the greatest loss to me. I loved it so much for her sake. I scarcely remembered my mother, yet all that had been hers was very dear to me. Perhaps I might have been worse even than I was if I had not had this one shrine at which to worship.

It is born in us, and is a necessity of our nature to worship something, and my something was my well-nigh unknown mother ; but whatever softness there was

in me came from thinking of her. There
was not much time for thought, however,
when house-hunting began ; it was indeed
a dreary time.

My poor father worked hard at it, trying
to find a home for us within his means, but
nothing that he saw pleased him. How
should they after Kingsholme Abbey ?
He shuddered as he told us of the gawdy
curtains and carpets, the paper ornaments
in the fire-places, the wax flowers, the
many coloured chintzes and cretonnes upon
which his poor, unused eyes fell ; the chairs
upon which he felt it unsafe even to sit
down ; the beds, too narrow to lie in, the
mattrasses, which appeared to be filled with
shavings ; the stuffy rooms which seemed
never to be aired, and which invariably
smelt of washing or cooking.

Days and days he spent away from us
looking for some place where we could

make a home. Daily we searched the
papers for houses to let. How well they
all sounded on paper, and what delusions
they turned out. Our dear home was
advertized too, and before long we had an
application for it. Papa was away, so he
was spared what I felt. No one else would
do it, so I had to show the strangers all
over the dear old place. Every cherished
crevice and haunt their prying eyes seemed
to peep into. It made me feel sadly
wicked; I believe I could have done an
injury to any one of them as they calmly
criticized my household gods.

The objects which were so sacred to me
were nothing to them, and I hated them.
Yet I knew that I was unreasonable and
overstrained. What my father wanted
was to let the place, and these people
seemed willing to take it.

Well, they did take it, furnished just as

it was, and we had only a month to pack up and to find some other roof to cover our heads.

Ah! that was a dreary month. It made us all older.

Every day seemed to add silver lines to my father's brown hair, but nothing lowered his pride; he was as erect and majestic as ever, for all he was a ruined man. Poor father! yet I know he suffered.

He came home at last, and told us it was all settled. We were to go straight away from the country which we all loved to a London suburb, and we went.

It was a long and tedious journey, and we were all fairly worn out before we got to the end of it.

The boys had left Eton. My father could not afford to keep them there; all that he had to live upon now was three hundred a year, the rent of our dear old

home. Nearer London it would have let
for double that sum, but only idle people
who are not making money could afford to
live in such an out of the world place as
Kingsholme.

Well, we had left, and our new life was
begun. The boys were to meet us at Little
Newington Station, and accompany us to
take possession of our future home.

I wonder whether my father took that
house because of its name? "Devonshire
Terrace" was printed on it in large letters.
It was the middle house of five. There
seemed to be one merit only in it—it was
quite new, and therefore we had no one's
dirt to annoy us.

It had been furnished by its owner to
let, and had not yet been inhabited; for
the rest nothing need be said.

There was no smell, either of washing or
cooking, but in their stead that of fresh

paint, varnish, new carpets, and French polish.

I fear we were not a contented looking party. We had travelled all night, and were not in the mood to be in a good humour, even with a nice house, which No. 3, Devonshire Terrace, certainly was not.

"Oh! what a beastly hole," cried Bob.

"And what a queer smell," added Trevelyan.

"Papa, how could you take such a place?" asked Florence, scornfully.

"It is very unlike the Abbey," I murmured, dreamily.

"Oh! Lavinia, my dear," whimpered Lady Trevelyan, "what draughts! what draughts! the windows don't fit, I shall die of neuralgia, and the walls are *so* damp."

"It is only an overflow from the shoot," answered my father, wearily.

Every one seemed to forget that the trial to him was far greater than to us.

Old Lady Costelion held her head very high, as though she were inhaling the unpleasant smells, feeling the damps, and with every sense condemning the transaction, but no word escaped her lips, which were firmly set, and as hard as iron.

Poor Lady Lavinia flushed painfully as she saw her new home; and then for the first time I gave my thoughts and attention to her, and noticed that when the flush faded how pale and worn she looked, and how thin she had become.

Our rooms were soon apportioned to us and very closely we had to be packed in our small abode—there was, indeed, scarcely breathing space, but we had to make the best of it. There seemed to be literally nothing to do at Little Newington but to watch our neighbours. The boys stood with their noses flattened against the window panes all day long, looking across the small common which extended as far as the station, observing the passing trains, and the passengers alighting therefrom, and greatly disturbing me with their remarks; for Grandmamma Costelion had taken it into her head to instruct me daily, and her mode of teaching had not improved with her advancing years, though her lessons were delivered with dignity, and if I did not profit much from them, she without doubt enjoyed them vastly.

"I wish, my dear Miriam, you would take to the study of geometry."

"Geometry, grandmamma, what an idea; I don't even know what it really is."

"It is the science of extension, my dear, and is employed to consider lines, surfaces, and solids, as extension is distinguished in length, breadth, and thickness."

"Oh! Miriam," cried Bob, "look at that man's legs coming along here, how I should like to ask him who is tailor is!"

"Kino, probably," struck in Florence, "and, by the by, I suppose *you* will have to employ him in future, unless there is some one cheaper."

"I'll back you to make unpleasant re-marks against any one I know, Miss Flo," answered Bob, indignantly.

"Geometry is not only useful but abso-lutely necessary," continued Lady Costelion, taking no notice whatever of the interrup-tion, "without geometry how could astro-nomers make their observations, regulate the duration of times, seasons, years, and cycles, or measure the distance, motion, and magnitude of heavenly bodies."

"Grandmamma," cried Bob, "do you want the pattern of a new bonnet—you'll have to make your own now, I suppose; by

George ! this one is a wonder, you had better come and look at it."

But grandmamma's hobby-horse for the time being was geometry, and she turned a deaf ear to the subject of bonnets.

I did not want to hear anything about geometry, and I comforted myself with the certainty that my relative's memory was not of the best, and that she would have forgotten all about it by tomorrow—she was wont to tell me to make a note of what she had been saying to me, that she might take up the dropped stitch, and of course I never did anything of the sort.

"By geometry, geographers show us the magnitude of the earth, architects are helped in their constructions, engineers are assisted in their works ; military men can't even build their ramparts without it, or mark out their grounds for encampments, draw their maps, or plan their forts."

Florence was sitting at the back window, reading a novel.

"Miriam," she remarked, "do you think the people next door take in washing? What a lot of clothes they have hanging out in the garden!"

"I should think, my dear, they wash at home; it is cheaper. I suppose we shall have to do it ourselves, it seems to be the fashion in Devonshire Terrace."

"Why, Miriam, the man with the legs is the parson, and, by jove! he's coming here!"

"Well, now you will have the chance to ask him about his trousers," sneered Florence.

"Even in music you need geometry," continued Lady Costelion—the entrance of the vicar did not stop her, she merely made him her audience instead of me, which was some relief to me, though it seemed to render the poor man somewhat uncomfortable. It had never occurred to him to be entertained by geometry before, most likely.

"So you see, sir, geometry must be most useful," went on grandmamma, decidedly.

"Yes, yes, doubtless, doubtless," he answered, with a longing look towards the door.

"Your church choir can't do without it; they learn to express sounds by lines, that is, by chords accurately divided—they know that the chord which sounds octave is double of that which it makes octave withal; that the—"

"Yes, yes; geometry is a wonderful science; a most useful—er—er—I hope you like Little Newington!"

"Miriam, my dear, will you call your father?" said Lady Lavinia, coming to the rescue.

"Thank you, I should much like to make the acquaintance of Sir Charteris Costelion," replied our new vicar, hurriedly, as though he feared to let grandmamma get in the thin end of her geometrical wedge.

"Why, bless me! it's raining hard!" I cried, with sudden interest, "and all those dry clothes will be wet through; evidently the people don't know it; how cross they will be!"

"It shows your kindness of heart, Miss Costelion, to think about the little troubles of your neighbours, and what a pleasure it is to be able to help others, when such help is possible; it is wonderful what we can do sometimes, if we only try," and the vicar smiled benignly on me.

"Geometry," began grandmamma, but Florence cut her short.

"In fact, Mr. Radcliffe, you think Miriam should have gone in to tell them their clothes were dry, and that the rain was coming."

"Well—I think—"

But Florence did not want to hear the poor man's thoughts.

"See! they have found it out at last; Oh! How they are running! What a scramble they are having, they will tear their things if they don't mind—dear me, really it's quite exciting."

"Poor women, they will get wet!" said our pastor, kindly.

"Rain, rain, go away! come again on washing day!" hummed Trevelyan; but Sir Charteris here entered the room, and we were silent; even Lady Costelion ceased her geometry.

If there was one thing more than another that my father disliked, it was being disturbed, and next to that he abhorred visitors, so it was with anything but a

smiling face that he made his appearance
among us, although he received Mr.
Radcliffe, the vicar, with the courtesy
which his office demanded, still that very
courtesy was grave and distant.

" I hope you like your house," began the
poor parson, nervously, " we consider Little
Newington a very healthy parish; epide-
mics are indeed never heard of among us."

" No, the buildings are scattered; you
have plenty of fresh air on these commons,
doubtless, but its salubrity is, I should
imagine, about the only attraction it has to
offer," answered my father, dryly. " As to
the house, you see what it is, and need
hardly ask if I like it."

Now Mr. Radcliffe had been the only son
of a widowed mother, and they had lived
on unusually small means; and No 3,
Devonshire Terrace, seemed to him quite
a mansion.

For some years he had been a curate in
Wales with a miserable stipend, and then
had, what appeared to him, the great good
fortune to be appointed to the curacy of
Newington, a small town some two miles
distant from Little Newington; the former
parish having somewhat outgrown itself, it
was decided to make the latter into a self-
supporting district, and Mr. Radcliffe, much
to his delight, had been appointed the
vicar designate, and an iron church had
been erected as a temporary measure,
but after a few more years of toiling and
scraping, a real brick edifice had been built,
and Mr. Radcliffe was a full-blown vicar.

He was neither an elegant nor an elo-
quent man, but he was earnest and good.
His coats were rusty and ill-made, but a
kind heart beat under them; the poor of
his parish loved him ; the middle classes
were apt to laugh at him because he was

awkward, and his trousers were knee'd;
and the upper classes—well, none had
arrived at Little Newington previous to
the time when my father took up his
residence there.

This is, however, somewhat of a digres-
sion, and all we knew of our vicar upon
the day of his first visit was, that he was
a plain man, rather under the middle
height, shy and uneasy as to manner,
shabby and badly fitted as to dress, and
that his boots were very thick; but I
noticed that he had gentle, patient eyes,
and that the expression of his mouth was
sweet; no other beauty certainly could have
been found in Mr. Radcliffe.

But to return to the conversation which
my aside has broken.

The vicar glanced around—to him the
rooms seemed airy and large; the new cretonnes, with their bright colours, cheerful,

after his own shabby little lodgings in a much smaller house.

"To me it appears a very nice place," he said, still looking about him.

Bob turned towards me and made a wry face; grandmamma breathed stertuously, like a war-horse scenting battle, and Florence burst into a merry peal of laughter.

"Very sorry for your taste, Mr. Radcliffe, if this is a specimen of it."

"You must excuse me, Miss Costelion," he answered, the colour mounting to his pale face, "I don't suppose I have any taste; but to me the place appears bright and fresh and clean; and to one who has felt the pinch of poverty himself, and has been amongst the poorest of the poor, that seems all that is needful."

"How horrible!" returned my sister,

heedlessly. " How can you go among such people ? "

"If for no other reason, because it is my duty," said he, gently ; "but, believe me, we are often rewarded for anything we may have to suffer; under all the dirt and squalor I have come upon good hearts, and not half so hardened as one might suppose."

" Why should they be hardened ? People like that can't have many temptations, surely."

"Can they not ?" he answered, with his quiet smile. " Come among them, and see, Miss Costelion, there is plenty of work to do, even in Little Newington."

Florence opened her beautiful blue eyes and looked at him in pure wonder.

"*I* go among your dirty people !" she cried at length. " No, thank you ! I am glad to say I am neither a parson nor a parson's wife, and it can be no duty of mine;" and I am sorely afraid she mimicked him.

"I do not approve of ladies as district visitors," said my father; "they should be shielded from the sight of all degrading scenes."

"Yet, who can influence like pure-minded women?" pleaded the vicar.

"Well! I am not pure-minded, Mr. Radcliffe," laughed my sister; "I'm a very worldling. I like comfort, and I am not at all satisfied with the state of life in which I am at present placed—you see I have an inkling of my catechism, although I doubt if I have ever said it right through; and as to this house, which was, I think, our starting point—I hate it. There!"

A saddened look settled upon my father's face, and he rose and left the room.

" Florence," I remonstrated, " how could you be so thoughtless? surely it would be as well to make the best of things. We have a roof over our heads, at any rate, and that is something. You have vexed our father and hurt his feelings."

For the moment I had forgotten the presence of the vicar, and I felt called upon to offer some explanation of my words.

" Trouble comes to every one sooner or later, I suppose, Mr. Radcliffe; to us it has come early, and perhaps it is easier to bear when one is young and strong. I feel it must be worse for my father than for any of us, coming to him late. If you had seen our beautiful dear old home, however, you would not wonder that Florence is dissatisfied. Sometimes I sit now looking over this bare common, with no land-mark but the geese to break the monotony, and think of the dear old Abbey with its grey stone all ivy-clad, its flowering myrtles, and its orange and citron blossoms, its soft green slopes, its tangled undergrowth, and rugged many-hued rocks and golden shingly shore, and I can almost imagine the soft sea breeze is upon my cheeks, the salt upon my lips—so powerful is fancy?"

"Your home must have been quite a picture," he said, with kindling eyes, "I have seen beautiful places and lovely scenery in Wales."

"Our home was an idyl; nothing could surpass it, I am sure; and it lay in England's garden, Devonshire. We had the open sea ever before us; one can *think* looking out over its broad expanse—within four walls one's ideas get cramped."

"Yet our greatest authors have written their best works in crowded cities, with the din of the traffic as an accompaniment."

" I do not think I could," I answered ; " I always feel as though my fancies were gathered from the sounds and scenes around me; the tinting of a cloud will colour a poem, I feel sure, or the breath of the wind."

" Miriam always was a star-gazer," said Florence, with a stifled yawn.

" She has brains, at all events, Miss Flo, and that is more than you can say for yourself," snapped Bob, who did not care to hear me run down, being his own sister.

"Of what use are brains to women ?" asked my sister. " Now, if Miriam had been a man she would doubtless have got on, as it is "—she shrugged her shoulders as a conclusion to her speech.

" As it is," I echoed, " I hope to find them of some little use by and bye. We have lost our money in this wretched bank failure, and I trust to earn enough by my pen to *keep myself* at any rate."

"Girls had better get married," remarked Trevelyan, with a grin, "then their husbands have to keep them, don't you see?"

"Boys had better talk about what they understand," answered Florence, hotly. "Grandmamma, I wish you would box his ears, he richly deserves it. I would, only his head is so hard I might hurt myself more than him."

Grandmamma had not been listening to us, she was thinking of other things, and self-absorbed; but now she looked up.

"You were talking of these houses, my dear, were you not? Do I like or admire them? Of course I do neither. As for the architect who planned them, it is very easy to see that he had never learnt geometry."

" Oh ! grandmamma, I hoped you had forgotten that," said Florence, crossly. " I have heard you dinning it into Miriam's ears until I really don't know what I have been reading."

" It is from this science that architects *must* derive their just measurements," continued Lady Costelion, sternly. " Now look at this room : a perpendicular is a right line which falls upon, or is raised from, another, making the angles on each side of it equal. Can you find me a perpendicular line here ? I have a correct eye, and I tell you there is not a straight wall in the house."

" We're like the leaning tower of Pisa, gran, I suppose," said Bob ; " but it's nearly as good as being back at Eton to hear you lecture."

" Would you like some Eton salt to make holy water of, Mr. Radcliffe ? " asked Trevelyan, irreverently.

"I don't think I understand you," answered the vicar, looking at him kindly, "it is some school joke, I suppose."

"No; it is not quite that," said Bob; "it is asserted that in former days, in papal times, the Pope gave an exclusive grant to Eton College to sell consecrated salt for making holy water; but very likely it may not be true."

"Dear me! I had no idea that holy water was salt; but I conclude it must be, or there would have been no ground for the tradition," said the vicar. "I suppose you like Eton. I have always wished to attend the Montem, but have never been able to do so."

"It is of no use to go unless you have your pocket well lined; everybody has to 'stump up,' you know," Trevelyan blurted out; "have you ever heard the verse about it?

" Each passing traveller must halt,
    Must pay the tax, and eat the salt.
    ' You don't love salt,' you say, and storm ;
    Look o' these staves, sir, and conform."

" We are not quite so bad as that in these days, though," interrupted Bob; " the Eton Montem is a quieter affair now than it used to be."

" I should like to have seen it when it was at its prime," cried Trevelyan, excitedly, " when the chaplain, after reading prayers, used to kick the clerk down the hill, and all that."

" That was a strange way to serve him," said Mr. Radcliffe, unable to repress a smile. " I am very glad I did not live in those days, and was not the clerk; and I am equally thankful that there are so few clerks left ; they were the most aggravating personages, echoing the clergyman's words a bar behind."

" Yes," said Florence, " the parsons are

quite tedious enough without the echoes, goodness knows."

Our vicar's colour rose, but he did not answer her; instead, he turned to Bob.

" I take an interest in old customs. I should like to hear a little as to the origination of the Montem."

" Would you like to hear about beating the bounds, then?" asked Florrie. " Do you know they *bumped the poor parson* the other day?"

" Yes," he answered, gravely; " I read about it, and that they were punished for it."

" Well, don't you know," said Bob, "there are so many versions of old stories, that it is almost impossible to say which is the correct one. I suppose we all believe in the one we like best."

" That is generally the case," remarked my sister, *sotto voce.*

"At any rate there is no doubt that it is a very ancient custom," continued Bob, "and that it derives its name from the mount which was afterwards called 'Salt Hill.' By some the Montem is said to have been instituted by the monks to raise money to enable them to purchase ground for the college. 'Salt Hill,' or the mount, being the first thus purchased. Others date it from the time of Henry the Eighth, and say nothing about the monks. It has doubtless assumed many forms since its first institution, but it has retained a semblance at any rate of the old ceremony. I have read many amusing accounts of the ancient Montems, and the ridiculous orations of the Boy Bishops."

"They could scarcely be more ridiculous than a speech delivered by the high sheriff for the county of Oxford," laughed Mr. Radcliffe, "of which I have read."

"Oh, do tell us about it," cried Trevelyan,

dancing about like a parched pea on a gridiron.

"I should be happy, but it might bore the ladies," answered the vicar, looking at us interrogatively.

"Oh, bother them," said my youngest brother, politely.

"Don't mind us, pray!" added Flo; "we may find it amusing."

"Thank you, I should like to hear it," I answered determinedly, for I was vexed to see my sister so rude.

Granny had relapsed into the transcendental.

"Well, it is a very short story," said the vicar, and can be told in a few words. When the sheriff arrived at the Mount of 'St. Marie's,' he thus addressed the Oxonians, being decorated with the gold chain of office about his neck, and his sword by his side.

" ' I have brought you some fine biscuit, baked in the oven of charity, and carefully conserved for the chickens of the Church, the sparrows of the Spirit, and the sweet swallows of Salvation.' "

" I rather like that," said Bob, with a grin.

" I don't see much in it," differed Florence. " Do *you*, grandmamma ?"

" I don't see anything worth looking at in it, if you mean the house," replied the old lady, wedded to her thoughts for the time-being.

" Now, we shall have some more geometry," said Bob, crossly. " Why could you not have left her alone when I am telling Mr. Radcliffe about the Montem ?"

" Simply because I am tired of it," replied Florence, with another yawn. " A year of Little Newington will send me melancholy mad !"

"I expect we shall have to send for Mr. Radcliffe to exorcise your blue devils before long," laughed Trevelyan.

"What do you think was the origin of giving salt?" asked the vicar. "It is an emblem of learning or wisdom, I believe."

"One of the old swells has left us *his* opinion in these words," answered Bob.

"'This rite of salt is a pledge or earnest which you give, that you will strenuously apply yourselves to the study of good arts, and as earnestly devote yourselves to the several duties of your vocation.'"

"So I suppose when the salt-bearers cry 'Salt, salt,' and ask thus for contributions, they pledge themselves on the part of the captain of the Eton scholars to do great things in the way of learning?"

"That is the way it points, I think."

"A point," remarked grandmamma, striking in, "is that which has no parts;

that is, has no length, breadth, or thickness, but as no operation can be performed without the assistance of visible and corporeal things, we must therefore represent the mathematical point by the natural one."

"Grandmamma was once a clever woman, a regular blue-stocking; but now she has reached her second childhood, and makes hobby horses of her former learning," whispered my sister, rather too candidly. "It is awfully trying, I can tell you, to live with any one whose mind is all angles."

At the term grandmamma started off again.

"An angle is the indirect course of two lines to the same point; or rather, it is the space contained between the indirect course of two lines to the same point, and there are many sorts of angles—a right angle and an acute angle."

"Yes, gran, and an obtuse angle," replied Trevelyan, laughing; "and that was what my master used to think *I* most resembled."

"Quite right, my dear, quite right," said Lady Costelion, approvingly.

"Do you think Sir Charteris is coming back?" asked Mr. Radcliffe, nervously. "I don't like to leave without saying good bye, but I have a service at five. I fear I have already intruded upon your time, and I can only say I have greatly enjoyed my first visit, and I hope it may not be the last. I only trust I have not been in the way."

"Oh, no!" replied Florence. "We have nothing on earth to do; we may as well pass the time listening to you, as in any other manner."

"You won't come to church?" he asked, hesitatingly.

"No, thanks; enough is as good as a

feast. I have been hearing you all the afternoon."

" You will understand my sister better when you know more of her, Mr. Radcliffe," I said gently. "We have all run wild in our dear old home, and have said whatever came uppermost in our minds. It has been a pleasant change to see a new face among us, and I am sure Florence thinks so too. And you must pay papa a visit another time ; perhaps we had better not call him back to-day as you are in a hurry."

So he took his leave.

"What a creature !" cried my sister. " Miriam, how *could* you be so civil to him ? Why, he told us distinctly that he had been reared in a pigsty ! And did you ever see such boots ? He must have borrowed them of a ploughboy ; and such a coat, and the knees of his trousers !"

"I was civil chiefly because you were so

rude, Florence," I answered; "though as
to that, one should be polite to every one
in one's own house; and, moreover, there
is something in Mr. Radcliffe's face I rather
like."

"Miriam!" cried my sister in disgust,
"what will you tell me next? All I can
say is, *I can't bear him!*"

"Whew!" laughed Bob, "if grandmamma were only following you she would
say you had gone off in a *tangent line!*"

"A tangent line," murmured the old
lady, "is—— let me see, Miriam, what is
it? I ought to remember; why, that is
the first thing I have forgotten to-day!
Ah, my dear, I fear my memory is going."

"Never mind, granny, I think I know
as much geometry as that," said Bob,
kindly. "A tangent line is that which
touches some figure without passing into
it."

"So it is, my dear, so it is; you are a good lad, Bob. Miriam is a sharp girl, too, but you are more of a Costelion. Charteris does not want my money—Bob, my dear, I think I shall leave it to you."

"Why, gran, you have none!" shouted Trevelyan, as though she had been deaf. "Have you forgotten the bank failure?"

She started and looked at him, then said stiffly, "My hearing is good, Trevelyan; you need not raise your voice;" and as she turned away there were tears in her eyes.

"How unkind of you to remind her!" I muttered, reproachfully. "Why can't you let her forget?"

"Ah," replied Florence, "it would be worth being in one's dotage to succeed in that!" and throwing down her book impatiently she left the room.

## CHAPTER III.

TREVELYAN stood in his favourite place at the window pane, beating an accompaniment with his fingers and singing snatches of a song of which he was fond, although he had been asked at least a dozen times to leave off.

As for myself, I had the power to shut my mind to external sounds upon most occasions when engaged in writing, but upon the present one my head ached, and I could not fix my attention, and my brother's noise worried me.

" There was a little man,
        And he had a little horse ;
    And he saddled him and bridled him,
        And then he rode across.
    Hi ! jingle, jingle, jingle,
    Ho ! jingle, jingle, jingle,
    Hi ! jingle, ho ! jingle, ha !"

" Is that song much longer?" I asked in despair; "I shall never get on with my writing to-day."

" Yes, ever so much," he replied, going off again briskly :—

    " And he rode, and he rode,
        Till he came to the seaside ;
    And there he saw a fisherman,
        Awaiting for the tide.
    Hi ! jingle, jingle, jingle,
    Ho ! jingle, jingle, jingle,
    Hi ! jingle, ho ! jingle, ha !"

" What doggrel!" I exclaimed; but I might as well have tried to stop a locomotive.

" It's a very pretty story," he asserted. " You listen ; it might do for a plot."

"Oh! fisherman, oh! fisherman
    Oh! fisherman, said he,
Have you got a little crayfish
    That you can sell to me
Hi! jingle, jingle, jingle,
Ho! jingle, jingle, jingle,
Hi! jingle, ho! jingle, ha!"

"Well, spare us the jingles, at any rate," cried Florence, covering her pretty, shell-like ears with her white hands. "There's no story in that, at all events."

But not even a jingle would Trevelyan omit; we had them all after every verse.

"So he gave the man a shilling,
    And took the little fish;
And he took the little thing home,
    And popped it in a dish."

"Rythm, rythm, Tre," I pleaded. "Do stop!"

"It is very pretty, my dear," murmured old Lady Trevelyan, nodding her approval, and keeping time with her head to her grandson's singing. "I wish my poor husband, the dear marquis, were here to listen to you; he was always fond of music. Lavinia, my dear, the boy takes after our family."

" Thank heaven for that ! " exclaimed Florence, earnestly, "and that there is only one child by my father's last marriage."

Our stepmother looked very near crying. "I do not know what fault you have to find with Trevelyan, Florence," she said, in a choked voice.

> ' And his wife came in the kitchen,
>    As she was wont to do,
>  And up the little crayfish jumped,
>    And near bit off her shoe.
>  Hi ! jingle, jingle, jingle,
>  Ho ! jingle, jingle, jingle,
>  Hi  jingle, ho ! jingle, ha ! "

" I think you might leave off knocking on the window, Tre," said his mother, timidly; "it really makes me nervous. Bob, can't you get him to stop ? "

"Shut up that row, can't you?" cried Bob, looking up from his book. "Of all fidgetting, that devil's tattoo is the worst."

"There's only one verse more," replied his brother, "and I shall be sure to go wrong if I don't keep time."

"Well, then, don't sing it at all."

"That would be a pity, when I've gone nearly all through, and grandmamma enjoys it."

"It's more than we do," grumbled my sister.

"Besides which, Miriam wants the plot to make a story of," and on he went again.

Bob got up to stop him, but I laid my hand on his arm.

"It is the last verse," I laughed, "let him finish it. If you both make a noise it will be worse still; and it will soon be over."

" He will begin another," he answered ;
but he sat down again.

" I don't think he knows another *all
through*," I replied, " so there is some hope
for us," and Trevelyan was already singing
lustily—

> " She hit him on the head,
>     And she hit him on the side,
>   And at last the little crayfish
>     Just laid him down and died.
>   Hi ! jingle, jingle, jingle,
>   Ho ! jingle, jingle, jingle,
>   Hi ! jingle, ho ! jingle,
>       Ha ! ! ! "

He uttered this last word like a war
whoop, and frightened his poor grandmother nearly out of her senses.

" Oh ! my dear, how you have alarmed
me ! Feel how my poor heart is beating.
Lavinia, my dear, you must correct the
boy ; he might have been the death of me,
he might, indeed. Fetch me a little sal
volatile, my dear."

"Red lavender is better," suggested Florence.

"Brandy is best of all! Take half a tumbler raw, gran, and you will be as right as a trivet."

"Nonsense, Trevelyan; how can you suggest such a thing?" I returned, with vexation; "it is disrespectful, to say the least of it."

"Oh, ho! How long have you taken to preaching, Miss Miriam?" he replied, making a grimace at me. "Since you have known and admired parson Radcliffe, I suppose."

"*I* admire him! What *do* you mean?"

"I heard you tell Flo so, I declare."

"If you cannot talk sense, I shall not speak to you," I replied, turning to my stepmother. "Shall I fetch the sal volatile for you, Lady Lavinia? You look tired."

I had never been able to call her mother.

That name, in my mind, was sacred, and could belong only to one—my own mother.

"Thank you, Miriam, if you would. I am not used to needlework, and it bothers me."

And as she leant her pale face once more over some mending which she raised from the table, it struck me how very pallid that face was, and how weary, and I fetched the sal volatile at once, mixed in a wine-glass, and administered it to Lady Trevelyan; then I took hold of my stepmother's work.

"What are you doing, Miriam, my dear?" she asked, fretfully. "I must finish it."

"I am going to finish it for you."

"You are? Nonsense; you have your studies and your writing. You have no time."

"I can *make time* for that."

"If you can make time, you might sell the patent of your invention for a good price, Miriam, and retrieve the fallen fortunes of the family!" grinned my young brother.

"I wish to goodness you were back at school," I groaned.

"You cannot wish it more than I do," retorted Trevelyan, "for it is as dull as ditch-water here. I feel inclined to go out and play marbles with the street boys."

"I can fancy the governor's face, if he saw you," returned Bob; "you would have a ride on Dr. Keate's grey mare, it strikes me."

"I wouldn't mind that, if I could only get back to Eton. What a jolly set of fellows they were!"

"You were always fighting when you were there."

"Oh! that was only to show our affection, Bob, and I shouldn't mind a fight now, to pass the time."

" No, I dare say not; but who on earth is this coming in at our gate ? "

" It is a demon visitor; and, good gracious ! what a queer old fish ! And here's a young demon coming after her, at a canter, and they have come out of number one."

"Surely these people are not all going to have the impudence to call on us," said my sister, haughtily. " What will papa say ? "

" Fortunately, he is not at home," I murmured, and in another moment our visitors were announced.

Our experience of society had never before introduced us to such people as Mrs. and Miss Rider.

It was quite useless for us to try and be stiff and courteous; we were all decidedly patronised, Mrs. and Miss Rider shaking hands with us all round.

" Let's begin as we mean to go on, my dears," said Mrs. Rider, heartily, " and I 'ope we shall be as good friends as we are near neighbours. I know all about you already. My 'usband's very 'igh hup in the company in which your dear pa is trying to be made chairman. Mr. Rider says he's not a man of business; but then, as Rider says, his handle counts for something, and the public like that sort of thing."

" I do not quite follow you," said my stepmother, civilly.

" Not foller me ?—you're off the line ? "

" Lady Lavinia does not, I think, know what you mean by my father's handle," I answered, smiling.

" What an innercent ! " exclaimed Mrs. Rider. " Where have you been brought up, my dear? Why, his title—his *Sir*, of course. Why, aint he Sir Chatterbox, or something of the sort? But, lor' bless me, I never had no head for names, and I took you for her ladyship at first; but this young lady don't call you *ma*, only Lady Lavinia, so I s'pose you ain't Lady Costelion, as I thought."

"My stepmother is Lady Lavinia Costelion," I said, going to her rescue, for she was looking most uncomfortable.

"Oh, that's it! But I always thought married ladies took their 'usband's names. If you'll look at my card, you'll see as how they've printed it ' Mrs. 'Enry Rider '— not ' Mrs. Sarah Rider,' you mark ; and ' what is sauce for the goose is sauce for the gander,' I've always 'eard. 'Av'n't you, Em'ly ? "

" Probably you were not a lady in your own right," remarked Florence, dryly; and

Trevelyan went into such convulsions of laughter that he nearly upset us all.

" That means, being the daughter of a dook, don't it? I saw the Dook of Cambridge once; a pleasant-looking man he was, too. So your father was a dook, my dear. Now, no one wouldn't never think it who set eyes on you; so quiet as you look. There's a deal more style about my Em'ly there."

" Lady Lavinia's father wasn't a duke, Mrs. Rider; only a marquis, so perhaps that may account for the want of style of which you complain;" said my sister maliciously.

" Very likely, my dear; but none of us don't think the worse of her for that, you may be sure, and a marquis holds a certain position of his own too; don't he wear a wreath of strawberry leaves when he goes to court?—I think I've heard Rider say so.

And how do you like Little Newington?
You'll find us all very sociable, quite a
'appy little family, as one might say. Nice
friendly *reunions* of an evening. My Em'ly
has a very fine voice, and likes it to be
'eard, so we has a good deal of evening
company, and I'm sure we shall be 'appy if
you'll step in. We don't 'ave suppers, but
a glass of sherry wine and a 'am sandwich
you will always find, and I know you are
musical too, for I often hear singing.
Some one was giving a nice cheerful *toone*
just now."

"You are very kind," said Lady
Lavinia, "but we do not go out now we
have left Devonshire; we have had a
good deal of trouble, and my mother is
delicate."

"Poor souls!" exclaimed Mrs. Rider.
"I heard from my 'usband 'ow you had
come down in the world, so I says to my

Em'ly, let's be just as friendly, my dear, as though nothing 'ad 'appened. Them bank failures is 'orrid things, but 'owever people can be so foolish as to put all their eggs in one basket I *can't* imagine. I says to Rider, 'Now you be sensible my dear, and place all your eggs in settings, and then pop 'em under some good 'ens, and you'll find as how they're all golden eggs, and will hatch into sovereigns;' and I believe he have took my advice; and bad 'ealth's a trouble too; and you don't look over strong, nor your ma neither."

"I am very poorly," replied Lady Trevelyan with eagerness," "I have not had a day's health since we left Kingsholme Abbey."

"Was that the name of your place, Miss Costelion?" simpered Em'ly; "how romantic it sounds!"

"Yes! that was our dear old home," I

replied dreamily; the brown rocks and the blue sea floating before my mind's eye.

"You should take 'op tea, my dear; I'll send you in some. I always keep a bottle filled ready, and the flannel is clean and fresh, so you needn't be afraid of it. A little drop of spirit warms the inside, and I've no objection to a glass of beer neither, but there ain't no fomentation in 'op tea, and indigestion is a mortal enemy, as I know, and there's many an evening I have to unloose my stays, and yet no one can't accuse me of tight lacing."

"Oh! ma!" said Miss Rider, "there's gentlemen in the room; you shouldn't."

"Gentlemen, nonsense, they wears them themselves, and that you may be sure."

Now considering the size of Mrs. Rider's waist, I don't think any one could accuse her of tight lacing!

At length they took their leave.

"Good gracious! what must she be like when her stays *are* unloosed?" said Trevelyan, leaning back helplessly in his chair, in uncontrollable fits of laughter.

"She is a very peculiar person!" murmured Lady Lavinia faintly.

"I hope the hop tea will do me good," pursued Lady Trevelyan.

"Why, there's my father at the gate; I wonder what he thinks of our visitors," laughed Bob; and then turning to me, "Miriam did you know that he was trying to get employment?"

"I know that he said he should do so when our misfortunes first came upon us," I answered, "but he has never mentioned the subject to me since, nor do I think he has done so to any one of us."

Then he came in and took an easy chair.

"Poverty makes one acquainted with strange scenes and strange people," he said wearily; "pray had that person been *calling* here—it is impossible that we can receive such visitors."

"I think so too, dear," answered my step-mother meekly; "Mrs. Rider is the most insufferable person I ever met in my life. She actually called you 'Sir Chatterbox,' and told me her vulgar daughter had more style than I have!"

This was too much even for my father's gravity, and he joined in the laugh which became general.

"But my dear Charteris, she really was very impertinent, and talked about our having come down in the world, and said you were seeking to be the chairman of some company over which her husband has influence."

"Dear me! you don't mean to say that woman is the wife of Mr. Rider? then, I am afraid it is a matter of necessity to be civil to her. Yes! I am seeking the employment she named. A Costelion will have to work at last."

"We shall be quite common people in time," groaned Florence, "appointments in the city, and friendships with the city men's wives."

"They cannot all be like Mrs. Rider," said Bob, comfortingly.

I did not speak, but I timidly slipped my hand into my father's; he looked at me for half a moment, and for the first time in my life, he kissed me spontaneously.

"You have good eyes, Miriam," he said softly," and I think I can understand their language."

"Do you really mean that we are to return this woman's visit, Charteris?" asked my stepmother helplessly.

"Yes, it must be done, my dear, I am afraid; Miriam will go with you. I am

surprised to find the man has such a wife;
—he is rather a decent sort of fellow himself."

" By George! here are some more demons;
carriage demons this time," cried Bob.
" I've had as many as I can stand for one
day—I am off."

"It is old Noah and his wives," exclaimed Trevelyan; "I shall stay to see
the fun;" and our little maid ushered in
a tall gaunt old man in a long black over-
coat.

There was a green patch over one eye,
and his mouth was much drawn on one side.
He wore shoes and white stockings, and
on either side of him stood a little old
lady holding his arm, dressed in the regular
pelisse of former days, made of rich black
satin and trimmed with fur, although the
chills of autumn had not yet overtaken us.
Around their sweet old faces were pure

white caps inside their cottage bonnets.
One, especially, I remarked, for although
certainly over seventy years of age, her
complexion was pink and white as that of
a girl.

What a contrast to Mrs. Rider!

Although so antiquated and wedded to
their own ways, it was easy to see at first
sight that Mr. Montague and his sisters
were of gentle birth.

The two old ladies dropped us each a
comprehensive curtesy, and then turned
to help the gaunt old gentleman to a chair.

"My brother's eyesight is not so good as
it was," explained one of the sisters simply,
seating herself near him; "indeed since
our family has been so broken up, we have
wellnigh giving up visiting; but we heard
of you through some very dear old friends
of ours who have been neighbours of yours
for many years—Colonel and Mrs. Arm-

strong. They wrote most affectionately of one of the young ladies—Miriam. Was not that the name, sister?"

"Oh! I am so glad to have news of them," I exclaimed eagerly. "They were so very kind to me; yes! Miss Montague, their son saved my life. I shall ever think of them with gratitude."

My cheeks were glowing, and I was feeling quite happy, when all at once my eyes fell upon my father's face. I had evidently annoyed him, and I felt chilled; my pleasure was gone.

"Are they all well?" I asked timidly. "Will you tell them they are not forgotten." I could not for the life of me help sending them that little message.

"Yes, Miss Miriam, I will tell them what you say. I shall be writing shortly."

I longed to ask after my old companion, my preserver, Herbert, but somehow I could not. The words stuck in my throat.

"Are you neighbours of ours?" inquired my father.

"No, we live some miles away, but we were anxious to be among the first to welcome you, for the sake of the Armstrongs."

"We were seven," spluttered the old man, "and now we are only four. My poor elder sister was quite too unwell to accompany us, but sent her apologies by the girls."

Trevelyan was grinning broadly, and Florence's eyes were dancing, yet these old folks were so perfect of their kind that one could not make fun of them.

"Yes, our sister is quite an invalid. We cannot hope to keep her long. The death of the other three of our family affected her acutely; indeed I may say she has hardly got over it. She has never been the same since then, yet the doctor says she has no actual disease, and she does not suffer."

" Decay of nature," said my father quietly. " The human machinery will not last for ever."

"Oh, dear no, sir," answered one of *the girls*; "nothing of the sort. My sister is only eighty-six ! "

A smile played about my father's mouth, but he merely bowed politely.

" Does she ever take hop tea ? " asked Lady Trevelyan eagerly. " That is just how I have been feeling ever since we left the Abbey, and I have been strongly advised to try it."

" No, I don't think she has ever tried it. We are all teetotalers," replied Miss Montague (that is the elder one of the two present).

" Yes, Sir Charteris, we have none of us

ever tasted the juice of the grape, nor have either of us married. And we were seven," mumbled the old man.

" Dear me, seven, and all single," echoed Lady Trevelyan.

" Grandmamma Costelion would call that a heptagonical family," said Trevelyan in a whisper to Florence, but of course I heard him, and I am not sure they did not too, for they soon arose to go.

" The wind gets cold and the evenings close quickly in now. Brother, I think it is time we turned homewards." Then the two old ladies got one on either side of their brother, and after a struggle he was hoisted up from his seat. We all offered our help, but they said they understood his ways best, and would not be assisted.

" We shall hope to see you all at the Manor House before long," said Mr. Montague.

Then we all shook hands, the old ladies curtsied, and my father went out with them to the carriage himself, and stood there to see them off, the sinking sun glinting upon his grey hair.

" Well, papa, what do you think of them ? " asked Florrie. " I was afraid to speak lest I should laugh."

" My dear they are quite unique, but they are gentlefolks."

" They are sweet old things—that is the two old ladies are," I ventured to remark.

" Seven, and all unmarried ! " repeated Lady Trevelyan. " I wish they had taken hop tea—teetotalers too. Well, to be sure ! "

" Is anything the matter, Lady Lavinia?" I asked. " You look very pale."

" No, no, Miriam ; it's nothing new. I am tired, that is all."

## CHAPTER IV.

MANY other visitors arrived. All our neighbours in Devonshire Terrace called upon
us, but as none of them have much to do
with our story, it will hardly be worth
while to enumerate them. Suffice it to
say none were quite so bad as Mrs. Rider,
none so refined in manner as our old-world
acquaintances the Montagues.

In due course the visits had to be
returned, but it was settled that my stepmother need not trouble herself in the
matter with the two exceptions given.

At first my sister declared nothing would

ever induce her to enter the houses of such a set of vulgarians, but as the dull days dragged slowly by she altered her mind, and when I put on my bonnet she followed my example.

" What! are you going after all, Flo ? " I asked in surprise.

" Yes," she answered wearily, " the people are atrocious, but I may get some amusement out of them." So she went.

The houses and furniture looked very strange to us after Kingsholme Abbey with our rare carved oak and beautiful old household goods. Everything was new and over-bright in colour; but one idea struck me very forcibly, that all these middle-class people appeared very happy, and another was that they all talked about their own affairs far more openly than those with whom we had been accustomed to associate, and never for a moment seemed

to imagine that their long narrations could
be otherwise than interesting to their
listeners; they also discussed their neighbours with freedom. People, not things,
made up the sum and substance of their
conversation. In vain I tried other topics,
pictures, books, needlework; even the
weather flagged, although in every house it
was invariably the opening theme. One ·
thing I soon plainly saw, namely, that Mr.
Radcliffe was a great favourite among his
parishioners.

No one had apparently found out the
fact that our position in life being so
different to theirs it would have been
better taste if they had stayed away, and
not sought our acquaintance. Our import-
ance was evidently measured by the size of
our house, which was undoubtedly smaller
than those of many of our new would-be
friends. Their chief feeling appeared to be

sympathy and a sort of pity for us as broken-down gentlefolks. "Poor souls, they have seen better days," seemed to be the language of all hearts.

I tried to take it as it was doubtless meant, but it made my sister furious.

"Miriam," she said, as we turned home-wards, "I can stand anything but their pity."

At last my step-mother felt equal to go to Mrs. Rider's. Florence was told she might stay at home; but she declared she would not miss the scene for the world, and she accompanied us.

Mrs. Rider's drawing-room was a better and larger one than our own, and boasted of some handsome furniture of a gorgeous style. The blinds were down and the windows closed, and the atmosphere was somewhat stuffy. A smell of cooking per-vaded the house.

There were too many mirrors, and it was a mistake to drape their gilded frames with coloured tissue paper, even though it was cut in wondrous traceries and designs! Doubtless the intention was to keep off the flies; still the glasses would have looked better without it; also, I should have preferred to see a well-cleaned grate or a fire laid ready for use, or if the fire-place must be decked, a few ferns and flowers; but Mrs. Rider evidently thought differently, and had a marvellous haystack of white and coloured shavings, with sprinklings of gold and silver, and a very garden of sprays of artificial flowers in wreaths and tufts all over.

We waited, sitting there in state, for some time, then a violent scuffling began to take place overhead.

"That's one boot on," said Florence, as a sudden stamp was heard.

".And there is the second."

" Then she must wear Wellingtons," I replied, laughingly, "or perhaps Mr. Rider is at home."

" If he should be, pray be civil to him, my dears ; your papa wishes it."

The scuffling continued—down tumbled a lot of things—and Mrs. Rider's deep voice seemed to be scolding the culprit who had dropped them.

A vast rustling was then heard upon the stairs, and Mrs. Rider entered, resplendent in a violet moirée antique, which was not quite in keeping with the pattern of a crochet antimacassar upon one of her florid cheeks.

It was evident that we had found Mrs. Rider napping !

" I hope we have not disturbed you ; perhaps you were lying down," said my step-mother kindly, her eyes straying to the tracery impressed upon the face of her hostess.

"Well, yes! my dear, I *was* taking just a little *si-ester*, but I was awake before you arrived, as Rider he came home and disturbed me. He is taking off his London smuts, and then he'll come and make you welcome; and 'ow's the 'op tea doing? I 'ope the old lady feels all the better for it, I'm sure. I'm always glad to do anythink for anybody."

"My mother bade me thank you for sending it," said Lady Lavinia meekly, "and she thinks it strengthens her."

Here Mr. Rider put in an appearance, and I was surprised to find him a somewhat grave, well-informed man; yet there was an expression of cunning upon his countenance which did not prepossess me in his favour, and before the visit was over I had made up my mind that I preferred

the wife with all her outspoken vulgarity,
for there was an honest ring about her, and
it was not necessary to look below the surface to see of what metal she was made.

Just as we were about to leave, "Em'ly"
appeared. It was plain from her spot-
less condition (she was dressed in white,
with blue ribbons) that she had had to
robe her mother first, and then herself.

"Here you are, my dear," cried Mrs.
Rider, with conscious pride. "I'm glad
you've come, for her ladyship was getting
on the fidget to be off; but now you
will sit down and sing us something.
'Hever of thee' is a lovely *toone:* give us
that, my dear."

And Em'ly, without a particle of "*mau-
vaise honte,*" sat down to the piano, and
with a rich but uncultivated voice bolted
through the song asked for. It mattered
nothing to the young lady that her accom-

paniment was one crash of wrong notes.
Sometimes when the chords were worse
than usual she would recognise the fact
with a "tut" between the verses or a
merry shake of her auburn curls; but it
was evident that Em'ly was more than
satisfied with her own performance.

"There's a voice!" exclaimed Mrs. Rider,
in a stage whisper. "Em'ly would make
her fortune as a professional singer; but
there, her pa wouldn't like it."

"Yes! your daughter's voice seems very
powerful," said Lady Lavinia.

"To be sure it is, and there's more nor
one in the parish likes to hear her sing,
you may make certain. There's that nice
young man, the vicar. Now it do seem a
sin and a shame that he don't marry. He
is not very well off, to be sure; but there
are nice gals about who could put something into the pot and some fuel under it

to set it off a boiling," and her eyes rested on " Em'ly."

" Thank you for your song," said my stepmother. "And now, Mrs. Rider, we must say good-bye to you all."

" Not good-bye, my dear, only ' O re-vore,' as the mongsoos says. I 'ope we shall be good neighbours."

To my surprise during the whole visit Florence devoted herself entirely to Mr. Rider, keeping up a perpetual chatter with him, much to that gentleman's apparent delight ; and the next day my father was elected chairman of the company of which Mr. Rider seemed to be the managing man. Perhaps my sister's pleasantries weighed down the scale in his favour.

On our return home we found Mr. Rad-cliffe in our sitting-room with the two grandmothers, one on either side of him.

Florence began to laugh. " I hope you

are spending a pleasant visit," she remarked
sarcastically.

"Yes, thank you, I am very happy," he
returned. "Lady Costelion has been giving me a few hints on the art of speaking,
and no doubt I shall find them very useful."

"Oh! no doubt."

"And what have *you* been doing?" I
asked Lady Trevelyan. "What sort of
advice have *you* given?"

"Oh! I was feeling very poorly, my dear,
till Mr. Radcliffe came in; very poorly, indeed. I really was quite frightened;
quite alarmed, I assure you. I was so
tormented. I was trying to sit in the
garden, you know, and those horrible insects worried me to that degree that I
really got quite *vicious*. I can't tell you
the state I was in. I used the essence of
sandal wood, which Lady Woods told me

was infallible. I called Mary and sent her in for it; but it was of no use whatever. Really those creatures are *dreadful*, and coming upon the terrible rheumatism from which I have been suffering, I didn't feel able to stand up against them, as I told Mr. Radcliffe. You know I have so little power, when I put up my hands they fall down again; and Mr. Radcliffe took me in. He thought I should be better in the house; and I told him the doctors had given me quinine and sulphur, and he advised me to use ammonia; and so I did, and I am much better, thank you; and he has been telling me of a poor woman in his parish in Wales who was crippled with rheumatism, so that her hands and feet had no shape left, and were dreadful to look at; and yet she was always cheerful and happy, and thanking God for all his mercies to her. But, dear me, I can't see where they were myself;

but it is a pretty story, and it amused me; if only I could forget those horrible insects."

There was a smile playing about the vicar's mouth which communicated itself to mine.

"Dear me, they must have been something very disagreeable," I said, after a pause.

"Oh, dreadful! Don't they torment you, my dear? Ah! you are lucky. *Horrid creatures!*"

"But what *are* they?"

"Oh! horrid insects which fly about and bite, you know."

"Wasps?"

"Oh, no!"

"Bees?"

"Oh, dear, no!"

"Well, then, they must be gnats!"

"They were only midges, Miriam!" came

in grandmamma Costelion's voice; and the
words were thrown out contemptuously.

"Only midges!" echoed Lady Trevelyan.
"Only midges! They are dreadful creatures. They nearly took away my senses.
Their bites are the most *excruciating agony.*
I became vicious, I assure you. Didn't
I, Mr. Radcliffe? Ammonia is a wonderful
remedy, certainly; but sandal wood cures
some people immediately. Perhaps mine
has lost its virtue. It has been in my
medicine chest for many years. Lavinia,
my dear, when was it that dear Lady
Woods gave me that essence?"

"I don't know, mamma," she answered
with a wan smile, "I think it was before I
was born."

"Dear me, that is many years ago! why
Lavinia, you must be"—

I placed my hand over her mouth—

"Lady Trevelyan, you should never tell

the age of ladies;" for I had noticed a flush rising to my stepmother's face, and an expression of annoyance.

"Have you ever tried quinine and sulphur?" asked Lady Trevelyan of the vicar.

"Not mixed, I think," he replied gently, with a laugh lurking in his eyes.

"I am taking hop tea now, Mrs. Rider has sent me some; but the doctors told me to drink beer. It is rather vulgar of course, and one could not do it in society, but I don't think it matters here, does it?"

"Oh, dear no, not at all; I take it myself."

Ah! but don't you find it generally sour?

I always keep a bottle of carbonate of soda to add to it, if necessary; it corrects the acidity."

"And makes the beer taste of pig, dog, and jackass!" added Trevelyan, who had just entered the room; "and I have some news for your grandmamma, you mustn't drink any more water! An Italian physician has found out that there are small leeches in water now, which stick to the inside, and suck your blood until they kill you; they call the disease anæmia. My dear gran, I hope you have not got it already; you know you have been complaining of feeling poorly lately."

"Trevelyan, this is too bad," I cried, "that is not in England at all, and you know it; it was in Switzerland—Why try and frighten your grandmamma, you have made her quite uncomfortable already."

"I don't see, if they are in one place why they shouldn't be in another," he replied doggedly; " and if the Italian chap were to come over here I'll lay odds he would find them here too; but Englishmen are such fools they go about with their eyes shut; so if I were you, gran, I'd be on the

safe side and not take a drop of water. I
don't know if washing in it can affect you,
I'm sure, but I have strong thoughts of
giving it up myself; fancy getting into a
bath full of leeches, you know."

"You have carried your joke far enough,
Trevelyan,"—I said with vexation, "pray
leave off talking."

"Oh! I have a lovely railway accident to
tell gran about yet."

"Then you won't do it to-day, I can
promise you. Really Mr. Radcliffe it is a
dreadful thing to have two idle brothers at
home all the day long, they are simply tor-
ments, and worry us out of our senses, to
say nothing of the way they are losing
their time. I suppose there is no school at
hand one could send them to."

"There is none nearer than Newington,
and the class of boys who go there are
decidedly mixed—I do not think Sir

Charteris would like it for his sons, but—"
the colour mounted to his face, and he
continued with hesitation—"*I* could spare
them a couple of hours daily if they would
come to me and read—as a friend, of course.
I don't take *pupils.* It would cheer me up
to have young folks about me, and we
should brush up our Latin and Greek together."

"That *is* kind of you," I said, gratefully, "and it would prevent the boys from
forgetting all they have learnt; but are
you *sure* you have leisure for this good
office?"

"It won't be like Eton, but it will be
better than nothing," confessed my young
brother.

"Then you will come to-morrow morning;
I can give you from nine till eleven—we
have service at twelve."

So that was settled, and he went his way.

"He is a very nice young man, my dear," sighed Lady Trevelyan, "and most feeling, I can assure you ; he put the ammonia on for me himself, he did, indeed, and as gently a woman."

"He is not young, at any rate," said Florence; "why, he will never see thirty again, and I should think he is thirty-five. I wonder where he keeps his mother ; does she live with him?"

"I don't know, papa did not see her when he called—perhaps she is dead."

"It is very good natured of him to teach the boys," continued my stepmother.

"I suppose he likes it, or he would not do it," remarked my sister—"and now we have only the Noahs to call upon. I expect to find the manor house just like the ark ; but how are we to get there? mamma can't walk ten miles."

"No, dear! I don't think I could manage

*one;* we must ask Sir Charteris about it, perhaps if he called with you girls it would do."

Florence was standing swinging her bonnet round by its strings. "Couldn't we borrow a trap?" she said, at length. "Old Rider has one; there is a stable at the side of his house."

"That is not to be thought of," I answered, hastily, "where is your pride, Flo? we cannot accept favours of these people."

"We accept appointments," she replied, with scorn—"where is the difference? and our father was always called the proudest man in Devonshire; poverty and a dull life crush even the pride out of one, I think. I intend in future to adopt the Frenchman's system, who said 'Always I gives so moch trouble as I can, and always I 'pays vot little as I can.' Oh dear me, what a weary world it is." And my sister threw her

K 2

bonnet on the table and sunk into a chair, and I saw that her blue eyes were filled with tears.

"Come and get your things off, Flo," I whispered, and she let me take her hand and lead her from the room.

When we reached the one we shared, she flung herself upon the sofa and burst into a passionate fit of weeping, and for awhile I let her alone, for when I took her hand in mine she pushed me away. Poor girl! She was little more than a child—sixteen, that was all—and a spoilt one too.

When her sobs had lessened, I knelt by her side. "Dear Flo, what is the matter?" I asked. "Let me hear your trouble, perhaps the telling may ease it, and I may be able to help you, who knows?"

"No, no; what good can you do. Can you give me back the old life? that is all I want. It is breaking my spirit to live in this wretched hole. It seems to be nothing to you, but I cannot bear it."

" Do you suppose it is nothing to me ? " I asked, " do I not see the dear old place nightly in my dreams. Does it not come to me, each sweet familiar spot, with over-whelming memories which crowd my brain."

" I wish they did mine," she sighed, " I only long for it all."

" Florence," I continued, " do you remember that my mother lived, died, and was buried there; I used not to feel she was altogether lost to me when I could go and rest my face upon the green turf which covered her; then it seemed so real to me that we should meet again, and I almost fancied I could hear her words, ' Lord ! how long ? ' "

My sister sat up and stared at me. " What makes you think of your mother, Miriam ? surely you cannot remember her."

"I do not know, I have but indistinct memories; yet I feel that I really do recollect her."

"Fancies, without doubt—I might as well draw mental sketches of mine. Miriam, you are very imaginative."

"Do you *not* think about your mother then, Flo?" I asked, wonderingly.

"What is there to think about? her portrait was at the Abbey; I know what she was like, and a very handsome woman she was; and now I suppose our tenants point her out as one of their ancestresses. As to her grave, I conclude it is somewhere at Rome, but I have never inquired."

"I should like to know if I were you, sis," I answered, softly, "but the portrait was not left behind. Papa loved your mother, dear, even before he married mine, and he gave orders to have it packed and taken care of in a London storeroom. If we had had space for it he would doubtless have brought it here."

The blue eyes increased in wonder. " I didn't think papa cared for anyone much," she answered.

" Oh ! Florence, how can you say so ? he has made a pet of you all your life, and he is fond of Bob, too."

" Yes ! because he is his heir."

" Heir ! heir to what ? " I asked, sadly.

" Well, his name, and the old place, if to nothing else. I suppose Bob will have to do what his father did before him—marry for money."

It was all true, and Florence did not mean to be unkind, but her words jarred on me terribly.

" And as to me, the father cares for me because I am pretty. I am a regular Costelion, and he is proud of me—you are not, you see, Miriam ; you must take after your mother; have you no likeness of her? Fancy papa having had three wives! and I should not be surprised if he has the chance to get a fourth before long; Lady Lavinia looks awfully ill."

"Oh! Flo, don't say so."

"Why, Miriam, you can't pretend to care; you at any rate have never liked her, and I am sure papa has no affection for her."

"I should not like her to die," I answered, rather conscience stricken. "We have usually got on fairly well, and perhaps when we have not done so it has been my fault, and not hers; I do not think she has ever been unkind to us, Florence, we ought to like her."

"Oughts don't count for anything," replied my sister, "and we have never thought much about her; but I suppose if she dies you will canonize her, and we shall have one saint more."

" Pray do not make jokes upon such a subject as life and death, dear," I urged, passing my hand caressingly over her beautiful golden hair.

" Do you know, Miriam," she answered, with energy, " I think it is much better to die young, unless one is very happy. Fancy if one had to drag out forty, fifty, or even sixty years of existence at No. 3, Devonshire Terrace, with no one to speak to from year's end to year's end ; I had much rather die and have done with it. I would rather ' shuffle off my mortal coil,' and——"

" And what ? " I questioned, looking at her, reproachfully.

" Well, I don't quite know what after that," she replied, with an uneasy laugh.

What could I answer her ? I could only wish that my dear old friend, Mrs. Armstrong, had been near, for she would have known what to say in her sweet motherly way, to show her that such thoughts were wrong. I had a dim sense that our lives were not given us to be one long holiday and gala, but that we should strive to be useful in our generation; only I did not quite see my way, and I felt unable to frame my ideas into words. So I was silent.

# CHAPTER V.

THE summer had passed away. The autumn tints had been lovely, even at Little Newington, where the beauty of the scenery was certainly not a strong feature, and now the trees were bare and leafless.

November fogs had given place to December frosts, and the world looked white and pure with new fallen snow; icicles hung from the window panes, and bright fires burned in the grates.

Florence, my brothers and I, were alone in our sitting room—the former, with her slender well-formed feet on the bright bar of the far from handsome fender, was contemplating her pretty fur-trimmed shoes with satisfaction.

"Relics of the past," she sighed; "I suppose I shall have to wear plain ones in future."

"I can't see what girls want with all these fal-lals," remarked Bob, sententiously. "Why need they make themselves into such very expensive luxuries? *We* don't want fur round our shoes, and lace and embroidery upon our linen, and all the rest of it. Why, when my luggage went astray coming from Eton last year, and Miriam lent me a night-shirt, the bristles round the neck of it tickled so I could not sleep, and I had a good mind to cut them off, there and then."

"I am sure I am glad you did not," I replied, smiling at his idea.

"Well! I suppose I shall get used to it

in time," continued my sister; "but I would rather be dead than dowdy any day in the week."

"Florence," I cried, "you are always saying those things; it is very unkind of you, and wrong, too."

"I am always thinking them," she answered, wearily, "and it is no worse to express one's feelings than to experience them."

"I am not so certain of that," I replied, "and surely you should try and govern your thoughts; you are young and full of health and strength; it is unnatural for you to talk so."

"Are *you* so very happy, then?" she asked, scornfully. "You would have made a capital parson, you are always ready to preach."

"Come, that's unjust," said Bob. "Miriam is not a blue light at any rate, and it does not prove she is happy, because she tries to make the best of things ; it is a pity you don't endeavour to follow her example, Miss Flo."

Florence took not the slightest notice of his remarks.

"Refuseth to hear the voice of the charmer, charm he never so wisely," laughed Trevelyan, whittling at a bit of stick with his penknife. "Flo, I'm sculpturing you in wood. Do you recognize the likeness?" and he held up a horrible little figure head, which he had hacked into some semblance of human shape. It had nose, eyes, and mouth, certainly, but that was all that could be said for it.

Florence glanced at it coldly, as though it was unseen by her, and went on talking in the dreamy way which she had affected of late.

"I think," she said, addressing herself

to none of us in particular, " I think it is a
pity that the days of the martyrs are past,
then people had only to differ from the
religion of the period, and they could get
quickly out of all the weariness of the
world ; and, I suppose, then they would
have made sure of a good time by and bye,
and their names would never be forgotten.
Generation after generation would hear of
one, and if one happened to be very pretty,
artists would paint pictures of the sad
scenes, and everybody would look on them
with interest and pity, and praise the mar-
tyred one for being so brave and true. It
would be worth dying to be thought so
much of; here we are nobodies."

" Dear Flo, do not talk such nonsense,"
I urged, "there are thousands of martyrs
whose names are perfectly unknown to
us."

" They were not good-looking, then, you

may be sure," persisted my sister; "what a beautiful picture that is of the Christian Martyr floating down the stream; it really would be worth while to drown oneself to look like that, and go gliding down with the tide so gracefully. Fancy how the people would come and look, and wonder, admire, and pity one. Would it not be lovely?"

"Oh! very romantic and lovely too, no doubt," said Bob, brusquely, "only you wouldn't look quite so pretty, you know, if by chance you got *turned wrong side up.*"

Upon which Trevelyan went into fits of laughter, and my sister was very angry.

"There's no cleverness in being rude, Charteris, or in being vulgar, either," she said, severely; and it was only when she was very angry indeed that she called my brother by his real name. "It is a pity that you cannot speak like a gentleman, and talk sense."

" There are some subjects which won't bear talking of at all, Florence," he answered, somewhat sternly for him. " We have had quite enough of this death and suicide business ; and too much. If I hear any more of it I shall tell my father, and on that you may rely. You will go on in this morbid way until it becomes a monomania, and the end of it will be that you will make a fool of yourself, and we have pride enough left not to wish you to become a nine days' wonder ; a fine chance for the penny-a-liners indeed, and a nice prospect for you to be shut up in a lunatic asylum for the rest of your life, with none but mad people to associate with."

" They cannot be more disagreeable than you are !" replied my sister, trying to keep back her tears.

"Oh! if you are going to upset the water bucket, I am off," cried Bob, jumping up. "Come, Tre, let us go for a walk, we will take our skates; we may come upon water somewhere which is fit to bear."

"Oh! wait a moment," said Trevelyan, "I would not lose the present expression of Flo's face for the world. This carving will transmit it to generations yet for to come."

"Do it another time, old boy," said Bob, maliciously; "once seen it is not likely to be forgotten."

It was a way with my sister that when worsted in an argument, she passed over the fact unnoticed, and went on with other subjects, as though nothing had happened, and I often wondered whether this was because her feelings were not acute, or whether she had great power in hiding them.

On the present occasion she did not, however, seem inclined to talk, and I was glad to remain silent, for, like Bob, I was somewhat vexed by her persistent nonsense and morbidity; it jarred upon me, and I was glad that my brother had expressed his feelings on the subject, even though it had annoyed her. While we were sitting in silence, Mr. Radcliffe was announced. He often came to seek my small assistance, although my father objected to parish work; and there were sundry club books, the accounts of which I kept for him, hoping thus to make up in some small measure for the time he expended on my brothers.

Florence had been antagonistic to the vicar from the very commencement of our acquaintance; it seemed to have been dislike at first sight, on her part, and she took every opportunity of saying unpleasant things to him, which rendered him very uncomfortable, and which it was far from agreeable for me to hear said to a visitor, especially as I had a great respect for Mr. Radcliffe. Upon the present occasion she was particularly quarrelsome and snappish, and more than once brought the colour to his cheeks.

"This is a horrible place," she complained; "it is enough to freeze the life out of one. It was never really cold in our darling old Devonshire; don't I wish I could be back there! I never knew what a charming place it was till I lost it."

"Don't you think, Miss Florence," said Mr. Radcliffe, gently, "that, looking back, things always seem brighter and happier than even they really were. There is no life so pleasant but that clouds must dim our sunshine at times; in after years you may possibly look back at the days you spent at Little Newington, and think that, after all, they were not entirely unhappy ones. You have your father, and brothers, and sister, around you. The good God has 'set us in families'—that is, most of us. I never had any one but my mother myself, my father having died in my infancy. I found great joy in her love ; but now that she has passed away, I am alone in the world."

For a moment he paused, rose, walked to the window, and stood there, apparently looking out. He was thinking of his mother, and when he came back to us his eyes looked dim and sad.

" You see your life is a fuller one than mine, for instance, Miss Florence," he said, in a quiet voice.

" I don't agree with you at all," she answered, roughly ; "you have your work, your daily round of duty, I have simply nothing on earth to do. It is enough to drive one melancholy mad."

"Cannot you work too?" he asked, eagerly. "There are many poor people here who would be thankful for some clothes for their little ones, this cold weather. Those good old Miss Montagues have sent me a roll of flannel, but many of the women have neither time nor sense to make it up. Now, would you mind trying your hand at one or two little garments?"

"I am no needlewoman," replied she, coldly, "and have more than I can do to keep my own clothes tidy. Miriam, no doubt, will manage them all for you, if you ask her; she boasts that she can *make* time."

"I fear I already trespass much on your sister's leisure," he returned, the disappointed look dying out of his face somewhat as he turned to me; but I am always

grateful for any help given to my poor.
The Miss Montagues have promised some
blankets, and they will be very acceptable.
I often think at night, when I am snug
and warm in bed, how our poorer brethren
must suffer, without proper covering over
them."

" I'll defy them to have colder feet than
I have ; even my hot bottle does not warm
them," said Florence, petulantly.

" Many of them have not the comfort of
hot bottles," returned the vicar, his good
temper reviving. Who could long be angry
with our spoilt child ?

" Then why have they not ? " she demanded. " An old bottle is not a very
expensive luxury, and water is plentiful
enough."

" But coals are not," he replied, " and
hot water cannot be obtained without a
good fire. However, it is as bad for you

to have cold feet as for them, as you remark, and since your hot application does not succeed, why not go on the other tack? I saw an account given of a cure for cold feet in a medical journal, which advised the dipping them, when chilled, into *cold* water for a short period, then taking them out and putting them back again, to encourage the circulation; then they were to be rubbed with a rough towel till they glowed, after which you might wrap them in flannel and jump into bed."

"What an absurd theory," said my sister, scornfully.

"I am not so sure of that, Flo," I struck in. "When we had a game of snowballs in the garden the other day, how cold our fingers were at first, then they glowed so we could hardly bear them. Grandmamma would prove it by Euclid. Things that are equal to the same, are equal to one another, you know."

"Well, does it not strike you we might find a more agreeable topic of conversation?" asked my sister, discontentedly. "Now, have you not a little scandal to tell us? There might be something interesting, and even amusing, in that. I have always meant to ask you about Mrs. Rider. How came her husband to marry such a Goth?"

"Of course, she has no education," replied our vicar, "but I think her vastly superior in nature to Mr. Rider; he has the brains, she the heart."

"And who on earth was she?" asked my sister; "I never saw such a specimen of the species before—never; they don't grow in Devonshire."

"Mrs. Rider was just a common orange girl in the streets of London," said Mr.

Radcliffe, "that was all. She did not even know her own name beyond that of 'Sally,' nor who her parents had been; but she was an honest girl, and, in those days, good-looking, and an old merchant took a fancy to her, and married her. No doubt he would have had her well educated, but that he fell into ill health. Sally proved a tender nurse to him, and when he died, about a year after their marriage, he left her a nice little fortune, and Mr. Rider, who was one of the old man's clerks, proposed to the widow, and was accepted. Every one knew that he married her for the sake of her money, and that he cared little or nothing for her, but Mrs. Rider did not discover the fact, as he has never ill-used her. He has gone into various speculations since then, and promoted many schemes, and, so far, seems not to have burnt his fingers; but, I must confess, he

is not a man I could trust with any confidence."

" What a funny story," remarked my
sister; "one can hardly fancy a romance
behind that bulky form."

" Dear me! there is the church bell,"
exclaimed the vicar, starting up. "I had
no idea I had been here so long; time
passes quickly in pleasant company."

Then he wished us good-bye.

When he was gone, we relapsed into the
silence in which he had found us. I was busy
doing some needlework, and my sister was
gazing absently into the fire. After a long
pause she raised a pair of mischievous blue
eyes to my face—

" Miriam, I have made up my mind to
cultivate him."

" What do you mean—whom?" I questioned.

" Why, the vicar, of course," she laughed.

"It will amuse me, and it will not hurt him."

"I am not so certain of that," I answered, gravely. "Surely you cannot mean that you have deliberately made up your mind to flirt with the man?"

"Yes, that is just the state of the case," she replied, nodding her golden head, knowingly. "He warmed up wonderfully when he was trying to get me to work for his beloved flock, and I think some fun may be got out of him. I wonder if he has ever been in love; and how he will feel when he recognises the fact that he is spoons on Miss Florence Costelion! Don't look so shocked, Miriam, dear; I don't mean anything serious, you know. I am not the girl to marry a poor parson, so you may make your mind easy on that score. Two hundred a year, with the poor of the parish for society, and coal clubs and shoe clubs

for my daily topics of conversation, varied
by provident societies, would not be in
my line at all."

"Then why not leave the man alone?"
I asked.

"I *must* do something," she said, piti-
fully, turning her pink palms outward,
with a pathetic gesture.

"My dear little sister," I urged, "surely
you can find something better to do than
tormenting an inoffensive fellow creature."

"I don't know that," she remarked,
eagerly. "I saw his eyes light up this
afternoon: I want to bring out that expression again; I am curious to see how he
will look when he cares for any one. I
have never had an offer—I mean him to
make me one; it will be a new sensation,
at any rate. Miriam, has any one ever
proposed to you? Come, now, did not
Herbert Armstrong?"

"Florence!" I gasped, with burning cheeks, "how can you say such things! Herbert and I were boy and girl friends—nothing more."

"Then I don't see what you have to blush about; and if that was all, how came you to have all those stolen meetings? I wonder what papa would have said had he known."

"You are mistaken," I answered, more quietly. "I never met Herbert once by appointment; if we met by accident it was not likely I should shun him, after his saving my life."

"Oh, of course not."

"And if you think to silence me thus, Flo, you are mistaken. I think it will be very, very wrong of you to get up this flirtation. I am sure that Mr. Radcliffe is an *earnest* man. He will not understand you; he will think you serious in your encouragement."

" Of course, I mean him to."

" In fact, you intend deliberately to take away his faith in women, and to break his heart ; it is not a very worthy pastime, my dear."

My sister raised herself up and looked at me keenly, then began to laugh.

" If I shall be poaching on your preserves, say so at once, Miriam. I always thought it was young Armstrong, but if it is the parson, confess the fact—there is honour among thieves, you know. Shall I congratulate you ?"

" Florence," I exclaimed, in anger, " do not judge me by your own standard. I work for Mr. Radcliffe because he needs help, and I like him, but that is all. I should be glad to see him happily married to-morrow ; he can be nothing to me beyond a friend."

" Well, I am glad the coast is clear," she

answered, calmly, and picking up a novel that lay at hand, she began to read by the firelight.

## CHAPTER VI.

I could not sleep that night; the conversations of the day before wove themselves into strange stories, and when I dozed, tired out, I awoke with some vague terror upon me, and a sense of trouble to come.

Martyrs, suicides, and broken hearts I could account for, but there was an uneasiness in my mind beyond these which I could not understand.

I got up the moment the light began to creep around my curtains lazily, put on my dressing-gown, and commenced brushing out the long tresses of my dusky hair, which wellnigh enveloped me, and as I brushed I thought. The vicar's story of Mrs. Rider came back to me. She had the traces of beauty in her fat red face even now; her features, although grown coarse, were by no means bad. There seemed to be something about the Riders which troubled me. What was it? Then it came to me; the vicar's words began to peal in my ears like a chime of bells—not joy-bells truly. "He is not a man I could trust with any confidence."

That was the feeling which had come upon me when first we met, *the* something which I had not liked in his face; and my father was mixed up with this man!

Could I warn him? No! I had nothing definite to say; I could not go and tell him that I had an instinct against Mr. Rider, and that Mr. Radcliffe did not think him worthy of confidence. Of course he would naturally be annoyed, and think my interference impertinent.

No! there was really nothing I could do; yet to sit by silent, believing danger to be coming, seemed the conduct of a coward.

Well, perhaps it was but fancy after all, and the natural consequence of a bad night, that I should be low-spirited this morning. I would try and shake it off. Cold as it was, I plunged into my bath, the iciness of which dispelled all fancies, and descended with cheeks aglow just as the servants were stirring. The fire in the dining-room was, however, lighted, and greeted me with a fierce spluttering and crackling, and a thousand flying fire-sparks born of the popping wood.

When the domestic had taken herself out of the way, I sat down to the little writing table in the window and began at a MS.

which I was anxious to finish ; it was only a short story, and I meant to launch it when completed.

I knew it was but a tiny skiff to go out against the strong winds of competition, and there would be stiff and searching editorial gales through which it must pass, which might use it roughly perhaps, and which would sear and scorch it, or beat it with angry gusts, and take the wind out of its virgin sails. It was my little dove, setting forth over the world of waters—how would it come back ?

It was my tiny boat, going out across a troubled ocean, with a sea of difficulties before it—would it find a pilot to help its inexperience ? Was a harbour for it ahead, to the right hand or to the left ? It was done. The words of Herbert Armstrong were ringing in my ears—

" Miriam, if you will to become an

authoress, the power of writing is in you."

My little story was now complete; my days of writing for pleasure alone were over; for the future I would make literature the aim and object of my daily life—success my goal. Oh, if I could only succeed!

But somehow the hands that held the MS. dropped with the written pages into my lap, and my mind went back again over the past; the days that were gone glided once more before my mental vision, clearly and slowly. Once more I saw a girl sailing alone on a green, washed sea. The breakers came, all white-crested and wind-driven, lashing towards the bay. The girl failed to make her boat face the driving blast when the sheltering headlands were passed, and was obliged to turn back. Her dark hair had blown from its fastenings; but the sailor's hat was safely tied under her chin with ribbons of navy blue, and the dark serge dress seemed none the worse for the mist and the driving foam.

Then the boat became unmanageable, running before the wind like a frightened steed.  It was glorious sailing ; past all the well-known objects the boat and the girl flew.  Yes! there were the grey stone walls of the ivy-clad abbey—but the boat was far from land ; there was the old familiar landing-place—but how were those two small brown hands to manage the sail and steer it in ?   Still it must be done.

Then a rush of many waters—a mighty roar of ocean-waves, fierce rolling billows passing over a dusky head—long dark hair floating like tempest-tossed seaweed, a frail thread between life and death, nothing more—a wild clutching, a gasp—the salt waves in face and mouth ;   then the

blankness of death, silence, and uncon-
sciousness.

I shuddered as this slide passed across
the camera of my brain. Life is dear to the
young. Azrael, clad in his sombre, bat-like
shadows, a thing of fear.

A bright one replaced it, a dreamy picture, with one figure standing out in full
relief. Strong arms seemed once more to
clasp me in a warm, sheltering embrace, a
kind, earnest face bent over me, honest
blue eyes looked upon me with pity and
interest. Only two words were spoken, but
they echoed in my ears.

He had said, "Thank God!"

A sense of utter security and rest, all
anxiety, all care had passed away, under-
taken by one stronger than myself. Oh,
why must that beautiful picture vanish!

Sitting there with my MS. in my hands,
yet with all memory of the present

merged in the dead past, I drop the pages unheeded fluttering to the ground, and stretch out my hands to stay the vision ;— my lips move, but no words come to them ; I can only by gestures pray that I may not awake to find myself among the angry waters.

"It is half-past eight, Miss, will you make the tea?"

I start! my dream is broken, the kind eyes are gone; my grey colourless life is before me, and must be lived. I must e'en be as strong as I can, and take care of myself, and do my best for others too.

"Why, Miss Miriam, you're crying. What is the matter; can I do anything for you?" asks the little maid anxiously.

Crying! I raise my hand to my face—it is wet with tears.

"No, Mary, nothing is wrong, thank you! I was only thinking of a scene I witnessed years ago; I did not know I was crying."

"It must have been a very sad one, Miss," returned the girl with sympathy.

"No, no, it was the brightest one I have ever seen."

The maid stared at me bewildered, but as I smiled at her and dried my tear-stained face, she was satisfied, and went away thinking Miss Miriam a very strange young lady. Then mechanically I put in the tea, gather up my manuscript and proceed to read it carefully over—but my quiet is past; my brothers come whistling down the stairs—I do not wish them to know that my story is going out on probation, I apprehend disappointment enough without their jeers and laughter—so I slip my papers into the drawer, and take my place at the head of the table. The two

grandmammas and my stepmother breakfast in their own rooms.

"Down first, for a wonder," cries Tre,
seizing me by both ears from the back, and
blowing on the top of my head as a
matutinal caress.

"Oh! Trevelyan, I wish you would learn
to be less rough," I cry sharply, "see how
you have tumbled my hair—I hate to have
it untidy—one might as well have a young
bear for a brother."

"Thank you for nothing, Miss Dignity,
that's all the credit a fellow gets for being
affectionate—you should just see how some
fellows treat their sisters; don't care for
them a straw; never take a bit of notice of
them, I can tell you."

"Well, I must confess some of your
attentions might be dispensed with," I
reply laughing.

Bob kisses me, and sits down.

"I hope Flo has got over her fit of the blues?" he asks, raising his eyes to mine. "Why, Miriam! you've been crying. What's up?" Trevelyan immediately seizes me by the shoulders, and twists me round in my chair, and after an examination of my face he cries, "You've been blubbing, as sure as eggs is eggs."

I laugh upon the instant. "Well, of all the ridiculous boys that ever breathed," I protest. "*I* cry—now, am I one of the crying sort? You are both too clever by half this time."

"I'll lay my lucky sixpence upon it, and it's the only one I've got," persists Trevelyan.

"You know you are quite safe, and that I never bet," I answer scornfully, "you will have to grow a little older before you can see through a brick wall; now you only knock your head against it, when you come prying, and want to find out what is on the other side of it; so sit down and have your breakfast."

" What, before the governor arrives ?" he asks, grinning at me.

"Can't you hear him, coming, stupid ?" I retort, for my father's footsteps were audible on the stairs, but I must confess I had forgotten his absence in my endeavours to throw my young brother off the scent, well knowing his love of tormenting, and how my tears would be brought forward on all occasions if their existence could once be proved against me.   I rise to greet my father as he enters the room, and kiss the cheek he presents for my salute, and return to my place.   Bob regards me intently, but says no more ; he has the sense to perceive these remarks only harass me ; not so Trevelyan.

" Well, Miriam, we will refer the case to a higher court.  Will you be the judge, sir, whether Miriam has been crying or no?" he persists. Sir Charteris looks up from the newspaper, the pages of which he is cutting.

"Are you unwell?" he asks, not unkindly.

"There is nothing wrong with me, thank you, papa," I reply simply and pour out the tea.

Mary carries off three little white damask-clad trays, with the breakfasts of the elder branches of the community, and then re-appears with a fourth.

"Miss Florence has overslept herself, please, Miss, and will you send her her breakfast ; she won't be down for this hour or more."

Sir Charteris has soon finished, and starts across the common to save the train for the great metropolis ; the boys depart for their morning reading with our vicar and once more I am alone. From the drawer I take out my MS. I have gone over it again and again, but even as I read it this last time, I find little things that can be improved, left out, or put in. It is like pulling out grey hairs, there are always some to be found when you look again, but I had made up my mind that this was to be the last time of looking over.

A painter will stand before the picture which has grown dear to him in the painting, and touch it here and there again and yet again, darkening a shadow, intensifying a light, heightening a colour. To others it is finished, but to him never while it is within his reach, and his palettes are near at hand. He must turn it to the wall if he would get on with his other work, or send it away out of the range of his brush, So I lighted a candle, rolled the MS. into a neat little parcel, and stamped the wax with which I closed it, with the seal upon my watch-chain. We had no letter weights at No. 3, Devonshire Terrace, so having directed it to the editor of a well-known magazine, I ran up stairs to my own room to put on my hat and jacket. My sister was coiling the last golden tress of her hair as I entered.

" Will you come for a walk this beautiful morning?" I ask, turning to her as I speak, "it is very fine, and the air so crisp—just the day for a good long walk. I am going to the post-office first, and then we can take any route you like."

"No, thanks, Miriam, I have other fish to fry," is all her reply.

"You really won't come," I say regret-fully.

"I really won't; I am quite obdurate," she answers.

My things are on and I am ready to start.

"I am quite sorry," I say, with my fingers on the door handle; "won't you change your mind, it would do you good?"

But my sister only shakes her golden head, and I start alone, the little roll of papers in my hand.

At the post office I get it weighed. It will go for twopence. What a tiny story it is after all, yet my heart beats as I hear it fall heavily, heavily for such a short tale, into the box, with an important thud. Then I breathe more freely. Whatever comes of it, it is gone; I cannot get it back now. I wonder, as I walk along, when I shall learn its fate, and what that fate may be. Then I tell myself that I shall be unfitted for other work if I spend the interim in doubts and fears and wonderings, and determine to try and shut out the remembrance of the little packet from my mind; but first I fall to thinking yet again of

Herbert Armstrong's words. Is it possible that I really may succeed in time ?

Thus questioning, I come to cross roads. One leads direct into the town, the other, if followed, to Faresham, where on the outskirts of the village stood the Manor House, which had been in the Montague family for generations ; where the seven had lived their peaceful lives together, and where three of them had died their peaceful deaths. And now when these four shall have passed away the Montagues will be no more, for there is no heir to come after them ; and as I stood there remembering the fact, I almost thought that it was better so, for no new generation of Montagues could ever have been so sweet and innocent of evil as that which was passing so quietly and gently away. The Montagues and steam power could scarcely be co-existent. They could never move on with the high pressure of the nineteenth century.

Scarcely knowing that I did so I turned towards Faresham.

I had already returned the first ʿcall of the kind old trio, with my father and sister, and Lady Lavinia. We had at the desire of Sir Charteris hired a fly on purpose to do so, and I had walked over with my brother Bob since, and had received a most kindly welcome.

Perhaps it was the remembrance of that welcome which led me, as it were instinctively, towards the Manor House; perhaps it was the fact that the Montagues were friends of those who had been good to me in my need. Whatever the cause, I went, walking at a brisk pace, which made those five miles seem short ones, until I found myself before the handsome massive iron gates, with my fingers clasped around the old-fashioned pendant mediæval bell, which rang with such a deep tongued clang in the fine old garden, verdant, even in December, with its wealth of evergreen oaks and its rare, well-grown shrubs, which had been planted so many years ago. There the bay tree really flourished, flourished as I had never seen it do before; and the stately deodaras swept the ground with their branches, while the Lawsonias stood like gigantic sentries upon the soft green lawn.

The trees at the Manor House were of a very great age. Some had fallen from decay, but the old stumps had been retained, and were rendered sightly by being covered with the large leaves of the Irish ivy, which also grew in a rich bed under the spreading branches of the cedars, hiding the bare ground, which is but too apt to be found under those majestic trees.

The Manor House gardens were old-world, like their owners. No gem-like beds of brilliant flowers were ever there laid out in the gay spring time. Geraniums were grown in the conservatories, so were the calceolaria and lobelia, with the waxen-flowered begonia, side by side with the simple daphne, and the white trumpet-shaped flower of the datura overhead, and ericas of many hues, here, there, and everywhere. The walls clad with climbing roses, hoya, and stephanotis; while the delicate gloxinia peeped out amid the green leaves of the ferns, and the sweet scent of the gardenia was all around.

In the summer time, when I had first seen the old place, all these were in bloom, and the blue starred agapanthus plants stood among the aloes on the terrace, while the garden was filled with its old-fashioned flowers. Gorgeous peonies and ascension lilies stood side by side. Great yellow sunflowers were there with their faces turned sunwards; tall hollyhocks, China roses, foxgloves, southernwood, sweetwilliams, pinks, white and coloured, imperials, and the deep blue monkshood; the dark scabious flower, and beds of tender mignonette, pale blue and yellow lupins; all these and many more were there, while the scent of sweetbriar filled the soft warm air; but now only the white starlike flowers of the Christmas rose greeted me, and the bright red holly berries, which were plentiful that season; a bunch of mistletoe looked down from an oak as I passed under it, the wind blew a little gust and rustled it, and it swayed as though it laughed at me, and shook its white berries overhead. What did it mean?—that I was all alone, with no one to love me, none who came to kiss, even with the mistletoe in the boughs above, and Christmas near at hand.

Once again two words came back to my recollection—"Thank God!" Were they wafted upon the breeze borne from afar on the wings of the wind? "Thank God!" Oh! had he really cared in those dear days now so long gone by? Perhaps it had been so then, but that time lay back far away among the shadows, in the days when I was little more than a child. Now I was a woman, twenty years of age, with the realities of life before me—life and work. Day dreams were not for me.

I was soon ushered into a large, plainly furnished sitting-room, and was receiving the welcome of the quartette.

"My dear, this is an unexpected pleasure," cried the youngest, cheerfully, with a warm light upon her fresh hued cheek; "and all alone! Whenever I see you it reminds me of our friends the Armstrongs, the greatest friends we ever had, my dear."

"Perhaps you have never heard," the old man mumbled, "how Colonel Armstrong's father saved my father's life. He did, Miss Miriam, and his children can never forget it. They are both gone on before, his father and mine; but we love the colonel for his father's sake—for his father's sake."

"And for his own, brother. There never was a better man than Colonel Armstrong."

It was Miss Caroline, the youngest, who was speaking. Her voice was eager and her eyes earnest, and her small white hands were clasped and unclasped restlessly, as though she would keep down some overpowering emotion; and rosy red banners were hung out upon the still fair, smooth old cheeks.

What did this agitation mean?

Had Miss Caroline her own story, her own romance, her own sorrow hidden away behind that sweet, patient, placid face? Only one who loved could speak with that zither-like tremble in the voice. Miss Caroline was old, but surely, surely, her love was yet young. Yes, young and green, and fresh and true, or that light could not re-kindle in eyes long faded. Dear Miss Caroline!

How it happened I never knew, but I had slipped my hand into hers, I had stooped over it and kissed it—we had looked into each other's eyes—perhaps we had read each other's hearts, and from that moment we were *friends*.

Our compact had been a silent one; the little scene had been so quietly enacted, that none but our two selves knew.

The sight of those other three was far from good, they had noticed nothing unusual, and yet a compact had been made between us, which was to bear fruit.

For once I was absent from the lunch-table at home.

Everything seemed so peaceful, so real, at the Manor House—it gave me mental power only to sit there, and I had not the heart to refuse when they asked me to remain with them and partake of their mid-day meal—everything at the Manor House was solid, handsome, and sufficiently comfortable.

The furniture was chiefly of oak, grown dark with age—the floors of the same wood, covered in the middle with thick Turkey carpets, and the winter sun shone in at the coloured glass windows, all rose and golden hued, touching the sombre shades within with warmth and light.

"The best friends must part," I said at length, as the sun sunk low in the heavens, looking like a red ball of fire in the clear sky. "Will not the sunset be glorious to-night, Miss Caroline? How I shall enjoy it as I walk homeward."

"The frost will continue and strengthen, if we may judge by the appearance of the evening," remarked the second Miss Montague.

"Yes, yes; the sunset is very beautiful, speaking to us of a coming day which is all unseen by us," murmured the eldest, faintly, "but it is at sunrise that we grow weary, and ask for rest. I suppose after the darkness of the night and death's shadows, the soul loves to rise with the sunbeams. Angel's ladders! It must be beautiful to wake to new life with the renewed day. Do you not think so, Miss Miriam?"

Her words awed me. I felt somehow that she was "not far from the Kingdom of Heaven," that her awakening in the Paradise of God was not very distant, whether she departed hence with the rising sun or when it should be high in the sky, or even should the day be dark and dreary, and the shadows many through which she must pass.

Whatever might come, whichever it might be, looking upon the pure steadfast face, I felt that "all must be well" with her.

"Let me order the carriage to take you home, my dear," said Miss Caroline, "it is lonely for you to walk by yourself."

"Oh! no, I like it," I replied; "I shall think of you all the way home."

"That will not be a very engaging subject for meditation, I fear," replied Miss Caroline, with a smile; "and now I shall not let you go until you promise you will come again—soon—very soon, Miriam, dear." She held me by both hands and looked up in my face, and I stooped and kissed her. I was not very tall, not so tall nearly as my sister Florence, but I was far taller than Miss Caroline Montague.

"Yes! I will come. I like to come here so very much."

I felt all the better for their companionship as I walked homewards. When I neared Little Newington, I observed two figures who stood talking together—they parted, and each went a different way. I met one; it proved to be Mr. Radcliffe. He was in a hurry, he said, going to see a dying man; so he passed me with a word of greeting only. The other walked on slowly, and I quickly overtook her; it was my sister. "Why, Flo," I cried, "so you went for a walk after all."

"No; I have only been to church," she returned coolly

"To church! you? and on a week day," I replied, amazed.

"Is there any great crime in going to church?" she retorted. "Really, Miriam, if I had told you I had committed a murder you could scarcely look more shocked."

My sister had told me she meant to flirt with the vicar, but I certainly had been unprepared for this move.

"Florence dear," I said earnestly, "if you went to church because you longed for the peace of God's house, or for the comfort of His words, go, and may He be with you. I can well *believe* in such feelings; those dear old Miss Montagues would feel like that I am sure—as for myself I wish I could too; but I cannot. I go to church on Sunday because everybody goes—if every one stayed at home I should do the same; there is only one thing ever makes me *want* to be in church. On a Sunday if one remains at home, and your home happens to be just near enough to let you hear the sound of the organ, and the voices of many people raised in praise, coming all indistinct and wordless through the still air, one's heart feels too full for speech, as though it would burst—tears rush to one's eyes. You fancy you can hear the tune at times; as the voices rise you really do hear it, and when they fall you fill in the gaps mentally, and wish you were there with them, and feel as though you had been left outside Heaven with the gate closed against you."

"I cannot say I have ever felt like that," returns my sister coldly. "But I suppose this is only one of your wonderful prefaces, and we shall come to what you really mean, by and by."

Thus recalled to myself, I cease to dream and begin again. "I don't suppose I

express myself very well, dear, but what I
really want to say to you is simply this : if
you go to church for the sake of the service
go, by all means ; if, on the contrary, you do
so as a means to an end, oh ! pray, pray, do
not do it."

" You are rather vague, Miriam," answered my sister, somewhat superciliously,
" perhaps you would like to explain your
version of a means to an end ; you are fond
of talking usually."

" Well, in plain language, to try and
attract Mr. Radcliffe ; to gain his good
opinion, to enable you to work upon his
feelings, and to mould him to your wishes ;
to give yourself opportunities of meeting
him often and alone. There ! that is plain
enough at any rate."

My sister's voice rang out in merry peals
of laughter.

" Yes, that is plain enough, as you say.

Well, I hope you have finished your sermon
as here we are back again at this charming
Devonshire Terrace, I cannot call it home."

"But, Florence, you have not answered
me," I began.

"My dear, I never heard you ask any
question, so how could I answer? and I
am sure I have listened patiently to all you
had to say. I suppose you have done, if
not we can take another turn."

"I have quite done, thank you."

"Very well, then, we will go in."

Who could understand my sister? Not
I, most certainly.

That night, when all were in bed at the
Manor House, my new-made friend, Miss
Caroline Montague, sat down to write a
letter—it was to Mrs. Armstrong. This I
learnt in after years; but it is best told
now in its proper place. One of the para-
graphs ran thus:—

" Your sweet young friend, Miriam Costelion, has been with us to-day, and I have quite taken her into my heart. What a lovable girl she is, with such fresh, true feelings ; and what a happy man will he be who gains her affections. She does not forget your kind- ness to her, nor Herbert's rescue of her at Kingsholme, and speaks of you all with the deepest gratitude. From what I gather, her father allows her few corre- spondents, if any. Rest assured her silence is from no lack of kindly feeling. I am more than sure that none of you are forgotten."

This letter went down to Devonshire, and was duly received by Colonel and Mrs. Armstrong, and the next Indian mail carried it to their son.

## CHAPTER VII.

THE frost continued to strengthen, and daily our boys started with their skates in their hands over the surrounding country, seeking good pieces of water whereon to disport themselves.

I had managed once again to run over to the Manor House and see my new-found friend, and had received from her an affectionate welcome, which had left me with a warmth about my heart such as I had not felt since we left our dear old home. It is so pleasant to be loved!

My sister was going her own way. She

was supposed in our little circle to have become a "*religieuse*," and Trevelyan was for ever making side thrusts at her, referring innocently to "saints" and "blue lights," "Jumping Jehoshaphats," "Holy Moses," and the like, or saying wicked things; then pretending to see that his sister was present, and apologising profusely for his words.

One thing was certain, that Florence now never missed the daily services, fair weather or foul, and many a time our vicar would walk home with her, shielding her from the wind and snow with his large umbrella. He even took her out to teach her to skate—a fact which soon became talked about among our neighbours, and in time reached our father's ears; but it was with *me* that he was angry.

"Miriam," he said severely to me one morning when he entered the breakfast-room. "How is it that you allow your sister to go about alone? You are older than she is, and should take better care of her. Do not let me hear of her being seen on the ice again without you—mind that."

"I have no skates; but I can go and look on, if you wish it, father. Florence has none either, so I suppose she must have borrowed a pair. I would have gone before had she asked me."

"You should not wait to be asked," he returned, somewhat roughly. "*You* might be able to go about alone without remark; but all eyes are upon a pretty girl like your sister, and you should bear the fact in mind."

"I will endeavour to do so," I replied, quietly, but my heart was hot and sore within me. It had ever been so with Sir Charteris. Florence was alone to be considered.

Presently my sister came down. The look of weariness was not so apparent as it had been on her face, and in its place there was a restless, wakeful expression, and more than once her eyes turned to the grey sky and the slowly-falling snow-flakes which fluttered like large feathers across the window panes.

" You will not venture out to-day, Flo," I said, when greetings had been exchanged.

" Why not ?" she asked, sharply ; " the snow is nothing. Of course I shall go."

" Where is it you are going ?" said my father, looking up.

" Oh ! nowhere in particular," she replied, flushing over cheek and brow : "that is, I may walk up and see the skaters, perhaps."

" Ah ! in that case, Miriam had better go with you."

" There is no need for it, indeed, papa.

I have been alone before, and—and Miriam does not care for that sort of thing."

"Miriam, you have my orders," he said, decidedly, and went on with his breakfast. There were few words spoken during the remainder of the meal; the boys had already had theirs, and had gone off to the vicar's, and at length Sir Charteris started for the station.

As long as he was in the house my sister remained silent, but as soon as the hall-door closed she turned upon me with angry eyes.

"Who has been putting things into my father's head?" she gasped. "Miriam, is it you?"

"I have held no conversation with our father at all," I answered, quietly; "he has heard that you go out skating alone."

"But I *don't*," she interrupted; "Mr. Radcliffe goes with me."

"I doubt if he would think that mended matters, Flo. Anyhow, I have orders to be your shadow in future."

"I never heard such a thing in my life !" she cried, angrily. "It is scandalous, cruel, monstrous, abominable. I might as well have a keeper at once if I am to have you dragging after me always, listening to all I say, and prying into all I do."

"Surely it is still more unpleasant for me," I answered.

"Have you orders to go to church with me, too ?" she inquired, with a sneer.

"I do not know how far my instructions really went," I replied ; "but I shall not construe them so strictly as that."

My sister gave a sigh of relief.

"I suppose I must be thankful for small mercies," she ended, and turned away, to look out of the window.

"Please, Miss, there's no more water in

the cistern, and the pipes is froze, and none won't come in, and what is cook to do ?"

"She must draw some from the well, Mary, and fill the boiler by hand; there is nothing else to be done, unless you can thaw the pipes."

"We has tried that, Miss, but none won't come."

"Well, then, there is no choice in the matter, Mary; but tell cook to be very careful and put the water in gradually, as boilers are apt to break in these frosts."

We had a window at either end of the room, and in a short time I saw that my orders were carried out. Cook and Mary each went running down with an empty bucket, and came back slowly with it filled; so I dismissed the kitchen boiler from my mind.

"If it was not you, it must have been Mrs. Rider," said Florence, suddenly. "What beasts people are! why cannot they mind their own business?"

"What has Mrs. Rider done?" I questioned, preparing to leave the room.

"Why! she does not like to see Mr. Radcliffe attentive to me, so she makes spiteful remarks. No doubt she told papa. I will owe her one for that."

"I do not see what object she can have had in making mischief," I reply.

"Don't you? Have you forgotten what she said to mamma about his marrying, and how her eyes rested on her precious Em'ly?"

"No, I have not forgotten; but I did not know you heard the conversation. You were talking nineteen to the dozen with her husband."

"As if I could only do one thing at a

time, and *such* a thing as talking to Mr. Rider."

"You may be a perfect Julius Cæsar, for all I know, Flo; but now I must go."

Soon after, the church bell began to ring, and the slam of the front door told me that my sister had gone out.

When lunch was over she whispered to me, "If you *must* go, be ready at two o'clock."

"Oh! very well," I replied, more than half vexed that the afternoon would be lost to me; and I went up to the room we shared, followed by my sister.

"Miriam," she said, with heated cheeks. "He does not know you are coming; I dare say he will be surprised."

"Oh, indeed!"

"Well, I saw him after church, of course, and you know I promised yesterday to go to the lake this afternoon; but I could not manage to tell him that my family think I am not to be trusted, and that I am to have a sentry over me for the rest of my life, so I thought I would let your going seem accidental."

"As you please; but I cannot see how it matters what he thinks upon such a subject."

"I am sure I wish you were not going, Miriam, since you seem determined to make yourself disagreeable."

"Thank you very much," I replied; and Florence, having completed her toilet, marches majestically out of the room, down the stairs, along the passages, and opens the front door.

We have only one looking-glass in our room, and that she has monopolized during our conversation, so I have not been able to finish dressing; and now have to scramble on my things and hurry without dignity after her.

She has already got half way down the terrace by the time I reach the door, and I have to run in order to overtake her ; rather hard upon an elder sister, I think, but I make no remark, and feel that ere this, I ought to have learnt my lesson in humility, and not lose sight of the fact that she is beautiful Florence Costelion, and I only plain Miriam, with the blood of a plebeian mother in my veins ; as I reflect on this I pull my glove together savagely to button it, and tear it up the side.

"That looks nice, certainly," remarks my sister, "people will think you can't afford a new pair of gloves; you had better go back and get some others. Here comes the vicar, we will wait for you."

"No, thank you ; people will only think

right. This is my best pair, and I cannot afford any more."

Here we met Mr. Radcliffe, who certainly did look surprised and somewhat disappointed too; notwithstanding the fact that he smiled, and said, "It was an unexpected pleasure to see me." Poor man! no doubt he thought he was telling the truth.

My sister's spirits rose from the time we came upon him waiting for us, or rather for her, by the road side.

She laughed, talked, and was brilliant; her blue eyes sparkled, and his, so like a sheep dog's in expression, were fixed upon her as a dog's might be; wistfully, tenderly, love beseechingly, and were seldom removed from her face.

When we reach the lake, he introduces me to an old clergyman, who is very full of the restoration of his church; a work which is to be begun when spring days come, and I am, so to speak, button-holed for the afternoon.

It is very little use for me to have come with my sister, for she has flown away to the other side of the lake with our vicar's arm about her, and I have no more control over her than a man upon the sea shore has over a ship sailing away across the ocean.

I suggest to my old gentleman that I should like to walk round to the other side, but when we get there, like a Will-o'-the-Wisp she has gone somewhere else, and, tired and vexed, I take a seat beside my somewhat portly companion, whose breath is not good when walking, and listen wearily to his description of proposed pulpits and lecterns, reredos and screens, naves, and aisles, and transepts.

The church is a hundred miles away.

He is only a visitor in the neighbourhood. I am totally unlikely ever to see it, and it is to be wonderfully high church, and I don't think my taste lies in that direction.

"Your sister is a very good church woman, I hear, and I am glad, extremely glad, for Radcliffe is a really good fellow!"

I grow crimson.

"I do not know much about my sister's principles," I reply; "and I am at a loss to imagine what they can have to do with Mr. Radcliffe!"

"I really beg your pardon. I hope I have not been misinformed. I quite thought it was a settled thing."

"Does that mean that you have heard my sister is likely to marry our vicar?" I question, with increasing vexation; "because, if so, pray let me tell you there is not a shadow of truth in it. Florence is nothing but a heedless child, and the vicar must have more sense than to dream such a thing possible for a moment. He must be blind if he thinks my sister fit for any man's wife, let alone a parson's."

"Love *is* blind, my dear young lady," returned my companion, nodding complacently at his own remark, of which he was evidently proud, and thought he had said something sharp; "and no doubt I have made a mistake," he adds.

"Some one has made a mistake, most certainly," I aver, and then I rise. "Will you oblige me by telling my sister it is time to go home."

He looks doubtfully over the ice (Florence is in the very centre of it), and essays to do my behest, picking his footsteps with much caution, then, finding no serious results, he goes on a little more briskly, and the next moment my messenger is on the broad of his back, with his stubby clerical legs kicking, and his arms working, and he so strongly resembled a black beetle under similar circumstances that I could not move for laughing. The skaters came buzzing about him to assist him up, and among them our vicar, to whom, though shaken, he staunchly delivered my message.

"Oh! you can't want to go yet," calls my sister. "It is such glorious fun, it is a shame to lose any of it."

"I draw my own mother's watch from my pocket, and remark that she won't be in time for church if we do not return at once.

The argument is unanswerable, and the vicar's face assumes a grave look, and I hear him say, in a low voice, that he is glad I mentioned it, for in his happiness he had forgotten to keep any count of the time.

On the way home, Florence is again brilliant and sparkling. When we reach the church she stops. " Are you coming in ? " she asks ; but I decline, and bidding Mr. Radcliffe good bye, I pass on alone ; the afternoon may have been delightful to them, to me it had certainly been terribly slow.

That was, however, the first and the last day I had to look on at the skating, for the severe weather became more intense than ever, and we had such bitter cold as had not been equalled for many years. A terrific gale overtook us, beating the driving snow through the closed windows and under the outer doors, rendering us cold and wretched. The feeble church bell tinkled on, as modern bells are apt to do, lacking the silvery sound of the metal used in the churches of former times. The un-melodious " ting, ting," came borne on the

wintry blast; but even my sister did not
attempt to move, and only drew nearer to
the crackling log, and the blazing coal.

My father, too, was at home—vehi-
cular and railway traffic were well nigh at
a stand-still—the line of rail was deep in
snow, and all wise persons remained
quietly in their homes, if they were fortunate enough to have any. But what of
the starving poor, who have no roof to
shelter them?

Who can help thinking of *them* as the
wind beats with fierce fury against our
windows, rattling them angrily with its
powerful gusts, and making the nine inch
walls of our Devonshire Terrace house
quiver and tremble. The daily papers were
filled with sorry descriptions of the sufferings of man and beast. The anemometer
asserted the fact that the force of the wind
was not less than sixty miles an hour, and

in the hurrying gusts considerably more. Even the snow sweepers did not appear to offer their services.

The common in front of us was one vast mass of pure whiteness, a smooth surface without the sign of a human footstep upon it. The tradespeople left us to our fate. It was of no consequence to them whether we had provisions or no, and, like ourselves, they preferred keeping under shelter.

The poor postman alone, of all human beings, visited us while the worst lasted, and all this time our unfortunate maids had to draw our water from the well in the garden, and carry it in, or sometimes Bob and Trevelyan would go and do it for them, to save them a wetting.

We had a small bath room up-stairs; but now all baths, whether warm or cold, were denied us. The water for them could not be obtained.

More than once I had been down to the kitchen myself to remind the cook about keeping the boiler filled, and as often had received her assurance that it was all right, and she had drawn no water out—but something went wrong—what, we never knew. All at once, as we were sitting round the fire, a terrible explosion was heard, and the wall of our room was simply torn down, and my poor stepmother blown off her chair.

When we picked her up she was quite insensible, and without a word Bob turned to the door.

"Bob! where are you going?" I asked.

"For the doctor," was his reply, and in another moment the front gate had closed after him, and he was battling his way against the fiercely blowing hurricane. I gave him a grateful glance as he passed out of the room, and he smiled back at me.

Gently, we carried poor Lady Lavinia to bed, and did what we could for her, but there was a fixed look in her face which alarmed me greatly, and the nervous system of Lady Trevelyan seemed to be more shaken than ever.

Sir Charteris was tender over his wife, but there was no depth of feeling in his face —he was sorry and pitiful, and that was all.

The doctor arrived at last. What an age it appeared before he came, to us who were waiting, and yet, considering the inclement weather, he had been wonderfully quick. I asked for my brother, who had not returned with him, and about whom I felt anxious, and learnt that there was nothing the matter with him but exhaustion, the poor boy's strength being so spent that the doctor, Mr. Lyndhurst, had put him to bed, and administered a sleeping draught to him before starting.

"You are sure there is nothing to be uneasy about," I ask, looking into his kind face.

"Quite sure, Miss Costelion, and I will take every care of him, only, while this severe cold continues, I shall not let him return to you; he does not strike me as being very strong, How old is he?"

"Nineteen," I reply, looking at him, wistfully. "You don't think Bob is ill, do you?"

"No, he has outgrown his strength, that is all; in a year or two he will pull round;" and then he hurries on to the sick room, and I feel guilty in having delayed him so long. I follow him with quiet footsteps— poor old Lady Trevelyan leading the way with painful nervousness.

Mr. Lyndhurst does all that can be done for the sufferer, and once more I am standing looking into his patient, earnest face in the dining room; for the drawing room, with its brilliant hued cretonnes and chintzes, is a wreck.

"Is it life or death?" I ask, in an awed voice, trying to read his answer in his quiet penetrating eyes.

"It is both," he answered, slowly—"but can you bear to hear the truth about your poor mother?"

"Lady Lavinia is my stepmother," I replied, "I would rather know the worst."

"Ah! that makes a difference of course. Well, Miss Costelion, it is utterly impossible her ladyship can recover from the injuries she has sustained, all we can do is to alleviate her sufferings. We may keep her alive a year or so, not more."

Tears started to my eyes—I held out my hands as though I could ward off the approach of death—"Poor Lady Lavinia," I murmured, "poor Lady Lavinia."

"I ought not to have told you," he said,

regretfully; and then, as Sir Charteris entered the room, I slipped away.

I had no time after this for going out with my sister—my days were spent by the bed-side of my stepmother, and I did all that I, in my inexperience, could do; and indeed I thought but little of my sister and her flirtations; she and Mr. Radcliffe must look after themselves, if they were so foolish as to make themselves, or each other, un-happy, that was *their* look out.

Soon after, my father beckoned me into our third little sitting room, which had been given over to him as a study. " Miriam," he said, slowly, " my circumstances have somewhat improved since I have become the chairman of this company—that, added to the opinion of Mr. Lyndhurst, that these houses lie too low to be healthy, has decided me to move; and I have made an arrange-ment with my landlord to give up this house, and go into another belonging to him. Like everything else, there are disadvantages attending this change. We shall be much further from the station than we are here, but a small pony carriage will rectify that difficulty, and with a lad besides our two female servants, we shall manage. I have seen the house; it is detached, and stands in its own grounds; they are small, but pretty. You and the boys must take to gardening, and we must do the best we can."

"Is it very expensive, papa?" I inquire, with a dread upon me that we may be tempted in a larger place to spend more than we can afford.

"It will cost more to keep up, of course," he replied, evasively, "but the rent is reasonable; it is now being set in order, and will be ready in March; by then, Lyndhurst tells me, your mother will be able to be moved."

"Oh! papa, if we could only have Sham-rock back, since you intend to keep a pony," I venture; "we were all so fond of him."

"I have thought of that, too," returned my father; "I mean to write to the farmer to whom I sold him, and ask if he will let me have him back."

"Oh! papa," I cried, "it would be like old times to stroke his soft brown nose again! how I hope you will be able to get him."

"Do you think your mother is stronger, Miriam?" he asked, after a pause. "You have been very good in nursing her."

His thin, white hand was lying listlessly upon the table—a slender, aristocratic hand —I stooped and kissed it.

"I have done my best, papa, but I fear it is out of my power to do much good," I replied, gratefully; any kindness softened me at once.

"There, there, that will do!" he answered, drawing his arm quickly away.

"I have said all I have to say. I do not want to detain you longer, you may be needed upstairs."

"If I had been a sensitive plant, I could not have shrunk more quickly back from showing my feelings—my heart was beating —I felt ready to cry with disappointment and mortification, but I only rose quickly and left the room.

*          *          *          *

Before we quitted Devonshire Terrace, a rather absurd scene took place. Miss Rider determined to bear out her name, and sent into Newington for *a horse* to carry her.

My sister Florence, having heard from Mr. Lyndhurst of the pranks of a certain hack in the livery stables there, with malice prepense, recommended poor Em'ly to order that particular animal, known as "Harem,"

being the short for "Harem Scarem,"—
another horse, with a groom in wondrous
top boots, was to follow her, so that things
might be done in proper style. Up clat-
tered the animals, and my brothers and
Florence called me to the window. I did
not consider it particularly good manners to
watch our neighbours, but it seemed to be
the fashion in Devonshire Terrace, and I
went, not wishing to be disagreeable.

" Now we shall see some fun," exclaimed
my sister; "that horse objects to be
mounted."

" Oh ! Florence, how do you know that? "

" Mr. Lyndhurst was telling me some fine
jokes about him ; he is downright wicked ! "

" Why, I heard you advising Miss Rider
to ask for that especial beast."

" Yes ! that is where the laugh will come
in, my dear Miriam ; I owe her one for
talking about me ! "

"But do you know for certain that she *has* done so, dear?"

"Oh! I am *certain* of it."

Here Miss Rider emerged from the iron gates of number one, with Mrs. Rider and two maids in attendance.

"She *do* look beautiful," said the matron, eyeing her daughter approvingly.

Em'ly was dressed in a bright blue habit, and a brighter blue ribbon about her neck, with a bow of the same colour upon her whip handle. On her head was a Gainsborough hat, with an enormous plume of cock's feathers drooping from its ample brim.

"It is evident dear Em'ly thinks blue is her colour," remarked my sister, with a sneer.

"She is vulgar, of course," said Bob, "but she is not half bad looking."

At this moment the girl's foot was in the

hand of the groom, who was somewhat nervously saying, "wo ho" to the animal, which was standing with ears back, and tail tucked in, looking anything but a picture of amiability ; *his* horse being in the mean time held by one of the maids, at the very extremity of the bridle, but apparently it had not the faintest idea of moving; it stood with its head down, and its eyes shut, with bent knees, and an altogether weary look.

"Poor old beast! it doesn't want much holding," said Trevelyan, "it will hardly keep up with that vicious looking brute ; Miss Em'ly will have a certain amount of work with *him*, I'll warrant."

"She will have to get on first," replied Florence, with a laugh.

Two or three fruitless attempts at mounting had already been made, and both Em'ly and the groom seemed to be losing

their tempers ; no doubt it was galling to
them to be doing the thing so badly, when
the eyes of the whole terrace were peering
out, and *she* had meant every one to envy
her. Poor girl ! I could not help feeling
rather sorry for her, more especially now
that I knew this trap had been deliberately set for her by my sister.

The voices reached us from outside.

"You don't understand mounting a lady,"
said Miss Rider, irritably, "your master
ought to have sent some one who does."

"That's odd, too," retorted the man,
rudely, "*considerin'* I've been along of
'osses' all my life, man and boy ; and 'ave
mounted *real* ladies by the score."

There was an unfortunate stress upon the
word *real*, which made Mrs. Rider furious.

"Now, no imperence," she cried, "or back
you go, 'orses and all ; and your master
shall know the reason why, and that he

shall. If you know how to put the young lady on, why don't you do it? She'd better have a chair and get up herself."

"She's like a sack of salt to lift," growled the man. "If she'll only *go*, I'll put her up fast enough; on'y 'taint of no use for she to bounce when I've been strugglin' with her till all my strength's gone. I'll say one, two, three, Miss; and when I says *one*, you ain't to jump, nor yet when I says *two*, but when I says *three*, bounce as 'igh as you please, and darn me if you don't go up this time."

Em'ly stood ready, one hand on the pommel, and a somewhat large foot held up.

"*One!*" said the man; "there you go now, Miss, you was just a goin' to bounce, blest if you warn't."

"I wasn't going to do anything of the sort," protested Miss Rider.

" One—two—three ! ! !"

The suddenness with which the man uttered the last monosyllable, like a volunteer's word of command, was enough to waken the dead, let alone frighten a restive horse.

Poor Em'ly rose grandly with a fine spring, but when she had done so she had nothing to sit upon but the air, and she was rather substantial for such a platform. With a scream, she clutched at the groom's head—but alas! both hat and hair flew into the gutter (for Jerry Jarvy wore a wig), and Miss Rider followed them.

It was very muddy, the effects of the thaw after a prolonged frost, and it is impossible to say which was the dirtier when picked up, the hat, the wig, or Em'ly ; or who was the most angry, the owner of the wig, or the wearer of the blue habit.

Certainly, if Miss Rider *had* talked of my sister, *she* had had her revenge. Tears came to the poor girl's eyes. Tears of temper, I fear, for the mud was very soft, and she could scarcely have been hurt.

The two indignant persons stood facing each other. Jarvy, with his red, angry face, and a shining unfledged head, and poor besmeared Em'ly, looking heartily ashamed of her appearance.

" That reminds me of a riddle I've heard," cried Trevelyan, laughing—" Miriam, why is a bald head like Heaven ? "

" I cannot imagine any similitude whatever, Tre ; if Heaven is perfect, a bald head certainly is not, in any sense of the word."

" You give it up, then ? "

" Yes ; but perhaps Flo can guess it."

" Not she ; it wants brains to guess riddles."

"You're polite, certainly," retorted Florence, turning upon him angrily.

"Well, what is the answer?" I ask, trying to avert the coming storm—but Florence and Trevelyan are looking fiercely at one another, evidently intent on a row.

"Why don't you reply to Miriam, Tre ? instead of you and Flo staring at each other like two incensed tom cats," laughed Bob. "And there! I declare poor Em'ly is not going to have her ride at all " (for the last angry words had reached us, swelling up above our own little family disputes).

"Go back to your master, and tell him the next time I order horses, to send a respectable person with them."

"Thank'ee, Miss," replied the man, " he won't send *me* agin, and that I can promise you," and in another moment he was riding

the weary old hack home again to Newington, with " Harem " in high feather by his
side.

And poor, dirty, mud-grimed Miss Rider
turned sulkily into the house, with tears of
mortification in her eyes, while her mother
followed like an angry old hen with all it's
feathers ruffled, until she looked twice her
ordinary size, and goodness knows that was
nothing insignificant.

The door was quickly closed after them,
but that did not prevent the sound of
sobbing from being borne through some
open window and wafted upon the breeze,
nor did we fail to hear Mrs. Rider's scolding tones ; and it was evident that now
the real object of her displeasure was out
of reach, it had become necessary for the
choleric woman to find another on which
to expend the overcharged state of her
system.

"Poor Em'ly," said Bob, "I am afraid she is having rather a bad time of it."

"I am very sorry for her," I replied, regretfully, "for all this need not have happened. My dear Florence, when will you learn wisdom? believe me, practical jokes are both bad and dangerous things."

To all of which my sister answered nothing, but continued to look out of the window as though she did not even hear me.

"She is doing the deaf adder dodge," remarked Trevelyan, with a grimace, "so you may as well save your breath to cool your porridge; but isn't old mother Rider just going it? That is what one might call a safety valve, I conclude."

"Her steam is up, certainly. That woman is a caution, and no mistake," laughed Bob.

"Mr. Radcliffe thinks her very kind-hearted," I say, deprecatingly, at which remark I am greeted with a duetto of merriment.

"He should hear her now," Bob suggested, giving my hair a little pull; "there never was such a girl for finding out people's good points."

"She does not trouble *me* much in *that* way," observed Florence, stiffly, still gazing out over the fields.

"Ob! the deaf adder is not so deaf as it seemed, eh!" and Trevelyan began one of his war dances around us, until we were fairly dazed.

"If you *could* oblige us by behaving like a gentleman it really would be a mercy," cried my sister, indignantly; "what must people think of you?"

"People! I don't see them; there is no one to listen to me, unless you count the geese."

"These walls are not very thick, Tre," I

put in; "our neighbours can certainly hear you."

"Well! and suppose they can, what harm am I doing?"

"No *harm*, but—"

"There, Miriam, shut up, there's a good girl, you ought to like to see a fellow jolly. Now do let me sing you a song. You havn't heard 'Verbs and Tenses' yet. It's awfully good, but unfortunately I only know bits of it. I wish I could give it to you all through."

"*I* don't, Tre. Have you forgotten your mother? there is too much noise for her altogether, so do be quiet, there's a good boy."

"You are a regular wet blanket, Miriam," he complained; "a fellow may not say his soul is his own, according to you. But come now, I will return good for evil. I know you are dying to hear the answer to the riddle, and I will tell it to you."

"That is very kind of you," I laughed, "but I had forgotten all about it."

"That *is* a big one," returned my young brother, "you do not expect me to believe *that*. Women and girls are always inquisitive."

"Are they? You must be a good judge, Tre; your experience of the sex is quite unlimited."

"Em'ly's left off now," said Bob.

"You seem quite fond of Miss Rider," sneered Florence.

"Well! at any rate, I don't like to hear her cry," returned my brother; "a woman's tears always tickle me up."

"How precocious!" drawled she; "we shall be asked to receive the sweet creature as a member of our family next, I suppose."

"I do not think you will," he returned, quietly.

"All this began with my saying Mrs.

Rider is kind-hearted," I laughed. "I shall be afraid to assert anything another time if I am to arouse such a wasp's nest."

"Call us *hornets* while you are about it," suggested Tre. "Go on, Miriam, we *like* to hear you."

"Very well, then, I will proceed with my defence of Mrs. Rider. I contend she may be perfectly kind-hearted, and yet have a bad temper."

"Yes, she may, and again she may not."

"*You* may not think the two compatible, but really they are. Passionate people have generally generous natures, and will do anything for you when the fit is over."

"Quite so! oh yes!—cut your throat one moment, and kiss the place to make it well the next. Go it Miriam!" cried Trevelyan.

"I would rather have to deal with a person like that, than one with a sulky disposition, or even with a tormenting imp like you," I end, half in fun, half in anger.

"I have a very good mind not to give you the answer to that riddle now."

"As you please, Tre."

"Well, it isn't for your sake, mind, but it is hard that the others should be punished for you."

"Oh! don't mind me," said Bob, with his honest smile.

"That is all very well," resumed Trevelyan, "but Florence wants to know," and he looked for confirmation of his words towards his sister's beautiful profile ; but she took not the faintest notice of him or of his remark. Then the door opened, and a new idea struck him—by now he was really anxious to impart the solution of the riddle. "Oh! here comes granny ; *you* like conundrums, now, don't you?" he cried, turning eagerly to her.

"Conundrums? of course I am very fond of them; people often convey a very pretty sentiment in asking a riddle. I remember once a gentleman asking me why ladies, and especially I myself, ought to be very much afraid of lightning, and the answer was that they were *so attractive.* A very nice compliment, and so delicately conveyed, was it not, Miriam? Ah! gentlemen are not so polite nowadays as they were in my youth! I suppose *you* never had such a thing said to you, my dear."

"No, Lady Trevelyan, never!" I laughed.

"I thought not! ah! times are terribly changed; in my young days all the girls were belles, and the men beaux."

"Oh! granny, granny! I am afraid you were a sad coquette in your youth, and I don't believe, really I don't, that you are much better now; but never mind, I'll forgive you. And now about this enigma, conundrum, riddle, or whatever it should rightly be called. Would you like to hear it? Of course you would, so I will go on. ' Why is a bald head like heaven?' "

" Dear me, Trevelyan, I did not know it was. I have not an idea; because— because "—

" Because it is difficult to know it is there when it is covered with that darkness which may be 'felt,' " tried Bob.

" No ! "

" Because it is in an elevated position," I suggest.

" Wrong again."

" Because all may get it and few do," proposes Florence, who really had awoke from her reverie.

" What duffers you all are," cries Tre, impatiently; " you had better give it up if you can't find sensible answers."

" I think they are *very* sensible,"

contended Florence, "and the chances are ten to one if the proper reply will prove half so good."

"Oh! won't it though?"

"I suppose it is something like a leg of mutton being better than heaven," Bob went on, reflectively.

"Then you suppose wrong, for it is nothing of the sort."

"Well! I shan't guess any more," continued Bob. "What is it?"

"Do all the others cave in too?" asked Tre, with a self satisfied, and very important air.

"Oh! yes!" I laughed, "I quite *cave in,* as you call it."

"Do *you,* gran?"

"I am not so good at guessing as I used to be, Tre, and riddles are not the same as they were when I was young."

"No! I don't suppose they are; we

make them by electricity now, you know, grandmother."

"By electricity! dear me, how very wonderful; where do they do it? I should like to see the operation very much."

"Ah! no doubt you would, gran, but they won't admit you unless you are a Freemason."

"A Freemason! then I won't go; they shall never make one of *me*, although I have heard that they did it to some poor lady, because she was listening to their dreadful secrets."

"Did what?" asked Bob, unable to restrain his amusement. "Do you know, Lady Trevelyan, Freemasons are most charitable people, and do much good. I hope to be one some day myself."

"You're very young, Bob, and don't understand these things," continued Lady Trevelyan, mysteriously; "but take my advice, and have nothing to do with them. Why! they are a *secret society.* They might ask you to *murder* some one you know, and you would *have to do it!*"

At this we one and all burst out laughing, much to the old lady's indignation.

"You mean Nihilists, not Freemasons, Lady Trevelyan," said Bob, kindly.

"Come, Tre, let us have this riddle," I suggest, in order to turn the subject. "We *all cave in;* we give it up."

"Because," began my young brother——

"Speak for yourself, Miriam," interrupted Florence. "I have no intention whatever of giving it up. I shall go on guessing. Because it is—"

"Well?"

"Oh! I don't know."

"You *do* give it up, then."

"I tell you I do *not.* I could guess it easily, but I shall not take the trouble."

"That is a very fine horse you are riding, Miss Flo! Take care it does not throw you, as Harem did Miss Rider," suggests Trevelyan.

"How could she be thrown from a thing she didn't mount, stupid?" asked Florence, over her shoulder, as she sailed majestically from the room.

"She has a sweet temper, hasn't she?" remarked Trevelyan, with a grin, addressing no one in particular, and looking towards the closed door.

"It is a pity you torment her so, Tre," I begin; but he will not hear me out.

"Oh! say it is me, by all means. Somehow everything is always my fault."

"But what is the answer, my dear?" demands Lady Trevelyan, unconsciously coming to the rescue.

"Well! now she's gone," he answered, with a nod of the head towards the doorway, "I don't mind telling you. 'Because it is a bright, shining spot, where there is no dying (dyeing) and no parting.'"

"Why that is as old as the hills," I cry. "I thought it was something new."

"Well, it *is* new, is it not? *I* never heard it until quite lately."

"But you are not every one," remarks Bob, giving him a slap on the shoulder, "and it's *my* belief that Noah made that riddle in the ark!"

"Did he really, my dear?" asked Lady Trevelyan. "It is a very pretty riddle, and its pedigree is most interesting. I did not know that Noah was a literary man."

"If that constitutes a literary man, gran, I'm one. I made a conundrum yesterday. Shall I tell it to you?"

"Oh! Tre, do spare us," I pleaded. "I have such a lot of work to do, and I shall never get it finished if you will not let me have a little peace."

" What, have you not finished those window curtains for the new house yet? I must say it is a shame that Florence does not help you. How many pairs are there?"

" Fifteen or sixteen. It is rather a case of the 'weary pund of tow;' but no doubt I shall get through them in time; and there are plenty of other things to be done besides."

"Poor old girl," whispered my own brother, softly, "I wish I could help you; but although Sir Robert Sale could use his needle as well as his sword, I am sorry to say I cannot. I can, however, turn the handle of the sewing machine, if that will save you at all."

" And I will devote myself to my grand-mamma's amusement," said Tre, with a

demureness which boded ill for her peace
of mind.   Then he began, in a low voice,
" I say, gran, there's been such a dreadful
shipwreck ! All hands lost."

" Oh! my dear, I can't bear to hear these
things ; pray don't tell me about them,
they make me creep all down my spine, and
I really shall be quite ill.   I shall be sure
to think of the poor souls whenever the
wind blows at night."

" Well, then, I will tell you about the
railway accident instead ; oh! gran, there
has been such a jolly smasher; almost every
one was seriously injured.   It was a race
train crammed with people, which came into
collision with the mail, and over a hundred
men were killed.   One of the guards was
blown bang up in the air, and there were
arms, and legs, and heads lying all over the
place.   Lots of poor creatures had their
noses broken, and their teeth knocked down

their throats; one man swallowed a whole false set."

Now, Lady Trevelyan wore a *set* herself, and this information quite finished her up.

"Good gracious, my dear boy, how very dreadful! It killed him, I suppose."

"On the spot! and all persons wearing false teeth are advised by the *Times* to leave them off at once. I thought you would like to hear the news, you seem to want a little cheering up. Well, Miriam, what on earth is the matter? you have been making faces like a chimpanzee for the last five minutes; want me to leave off talking, do you? well, why on earth didn't you say so, instead of making yourself so unnecessarily ugly? Why, I declare, dear Em'ly is coming in, accompanied by her 'Ma.' I'm blessed if there won't be a row at Florence having recommended them to order that horse; she will have to give her reasons in writing. I'll stay and see the fun out. I wish Florence were here; she's a great gun in the case of a row, she fires her shots mercilessly. Let us call her down."

"No, no, far better not; it would be most unpleasant for papa if we were to have any fuss with these Riders, when he is mixed up with the paterfamilias in business matters."

"Miriam is right," said Bob, "we must try and pour oil upon the troubled water."

"Miriam is a regular Mother Carey's chicken; she expels it as she goes, and creates a calm for herself; trust her to make peace, she does not appreciate rough weather one little bit," rejoined Tre. "How do you do, Miss Rider, did you have a pleasant ride?" he ended, turning to poor unfortunate Em'ly, who stood before us with very red eyes.

" You know as how she didn't," cried the mother, indignantly, "for you was all a standing at that there window and enjoying her discomfiture."

" Indeed no," I began, "we were very sorry to see that your daughter had so much trouble with that restive animal; the livery stable keeper ought not to have sent it for a lady to ride."

" There's others more to blame than him, and that's what we've come about. *Your* sister Florence, as you calls her, told Em'ly to *hask* for that 'orse, as it was the best ladies 'ack in the stud, and here's the result of her advice, and I've come to know what it means," cried the good woman, excitedly.

" It is very unfortunate that my sister should have given *any* advice," I answered, gently, "and I greatly hope Miss Emily is not hurt."

"Mother Carey's chicken!" giggles Trevelyan, aside.

"Nevertheless, we should like to 'ave it *hout* with her," blurted out the excited woman.

"I fear my sister cannot see you, I think she is lying down," I replied, colouring at the untruth, for I did not think anything of the sort; "and poor Lady Lavinia is so very unwell to-day that I am afraid I shall have to ask you to excuse me, presently."

"What a polite hint to be off!" says Trevelyan, in a stage whisper, which makes me redder still.

"Pray believe, Mrs. Rider," I continue, quickly, "that my sister never saw the horse in her life, and had your daughter met with any accident, I am certain she would have been as sorry as I should have been, and that would have been very sorry indeed."

"Well, my dear, you've a nice way of putting things, and I suppose I am bound to believe you, so I shan't say no more about it, though Em'ly's 'abit is completely spoilt—that bright blue won't stand mud stains, but it looks cheerful, and she 'ad it by my advice. And now, as you want to go and look after your 'Ma,' I suppose we 'ad better take ourselves *horf,*" and Mrs. Rider (like the month of March), although she had come in like a lion, went out like a lamb. And so long as we remained in Devonshire Terrace, poor Em'ly did not make another attempt at equestrian exercise.

END OF VOL. I.

STEVENS AND RICHARDSON, PRINTERS, 5, GREAT QUEEN STREET, W.C.

VOL. I.        S

www.ingramcontent.com/pod-product-compliance
Lightning Source LLC
Chambersburg PA
CBHW030801020726
47499CB00006B/1727